PRAISE FOR *T*

"Ami Sands Brodoff's stories ripple with wisdom and humour, alive with subtle observations and attention to the details of relationships. These stories range widely, fleshing out themes of mental health, family, and gender, taking us inside the minds of an experienced psychiatrist and a depressed teenager with equal empathy. These interconnected stories reach out for each other, forming a dense web of compassion."

—*Alex Leslie, Winner, Dayne Ogilvie Prize for LGBTQ Emerging Writers from the Writers' Trust of Canada, author of* We All Need to Eat *and* Vancouver for Beginners

"Magnificent. *The Sleep of Apples* exposes the consequences of being different, of risking tenderness, of illness and of grief. Ami Sands Brodoff speaks to the realities of our world in captivating and finely rendered prose that reflects the sure hand of an accomplished novelist. We fall in love with the recurring characters, we are haunted by their pain, we root for them, and celebrate moments of grace when they transcend the suffering that life flings their way."

—*Cora Siré, author of* Behold Things Beautiful

"*The Sleep of Apples* is such a powerful collection. Encompassing voices of loss, mourning, birth, and spirituality, an extraordinary group of interconnected characters work to discover their identities. Brodoff's writing is eloquent and illuminating. Reading these stories made me long to revisit them again and again. You will too."

—*Hasan Namir, author of* God in Pink, *Lambda Literary Award for Gay Fiction and* War / Torn, *Stonewall Honor Book in Literature.*

THE
SLEEP *of*
APPLES

THE
SLEEP *of*
APPLES

Stories

Ami Sands Brodoff

INANNA poetry
& fiction

Toronto, Ontario, Canada
www.inanna.ca

We gratefully acknowledge the support of the Canada Council for the Arts and the Ontario Arts Council for our publishing program. We also acknowledge the financial support of the Government of Canada.

Cover design: Val Fullard

The Sleep of Apples is a work of fiction. All the characters portrayed in this book are fictitious and any resemblance to persons living or dead is purely coincidental.

Library and Archives Canada Cataloguing in Publication

Title: The sleep of apples : stories / Ami Sands Brodoff.
Names: Brodoff, Ami Sands, author.
Series: Inanna poetry & fiction series.
Description: Series statement: Inanna poetry & fiction series
Identifiers: Canadiana (print) 20210271639 | Canadiana (ebook) 20210271698 | ISBN 9781771338813 (softcover) | ISBN 9781771338820 (HTML) | ISBN 9781771338837 (PDF)
Classification: LCC PS8603.R63 S54 2021 | DDC C813/.6—dc23

Printed and bound in Canada

Inanna Publications and Education Inc.
210 Founders College, York University
4700 Keele Street, Toronto, Ontario, Canada M3J 1P3
Telephone: (416) 736-5356 Fax: (416) 736-5765
Email: inanna.publications@inanna.ca Website: www.inanna.ca

For Michael,
and for
Tobias & Gabriel

So, you're born, and then what? ...
Hurtling through time, strapped to an explosive device, my life.

—Deborah Eisenberg, *Your Duck Is My Duck*

Quiero dormir el sueño de las manzanas...
Quiero dormir el sueño de aquel niño
que quería cortarse el corazón en alta mar...

Quiero dormir un rato,
un rato, un minuto, un siglo;
pero que todos sepan que no he muerto;...

I want to sleep the sleep of the apples...
I want to sleep the sleep of that child
Who longed to cut his heart open far out at sea...

I want to sleep for half a second,
a second, a minute, a century;
but I want everyone to know that I am still alive;...

—Federico García Lorca, "Gacela de la Muerte Oscura,"
"Gacela of the Dark Death," translated by Robert Bly

CONTENTS

WHAT'S MINE *Is* YOURS

Miri

When my fever hit 105 degrees, my father put me in the hospital. I remember coming home from my Bubbe Zelda's seventieth birthday party, shivering and sweating and aching all over. Apparently later that night, I was raving mad and didn't know my own name. I was eight years old, in grade three.

I'd never seen my father, a calm and collected doctor, so anxious. Dad hovered over me at Mt. Sinai and even stayed overnight by my bedside. There was very little that could make my father miss work since he was devoted to his patients.

Once my fever broke and I knew who and where I was, I liked being in the hospital despite my miserable flu symptoms complicated by a strep throat and that bone-deep ache. I didn't have to go to school, for one thing, not to mention I got all of the attention I craved. The nurses catered to me, and the doctors, who all knew my father, gave me vigilant care, telling their lame jokes and remarking on how much I resembled my dad, especially around the eyes. This compliment pleased me no end. Dad had magic eyes: hazel, changing colour depending on what he wore, with starbursts of gold at their centres. Early in my stay, Bubbe Zelda sent over a pint of maple ice cream, which I had for dinner. Best of all was having my father all to myself without another patient—of his—in sight.

Dad was a man of few words, but because I felt as if a razor blade was caught in my throat each time I swallowed and dissolved into a hacking cough when I tried to speak, he talked to me. He told me how much he'd loved to kayak on Kezar Lake in Maine when he was my age and how we would go together this coming summer, just us two, for a long weekend. He described the lake and the shivering reflection of the pines in its dark mirrored surface when the wind picked up off the mountains. He remembered the mornings, clear and chilly enough to wear a sweatshirt, how good eggs and toast cooked over the fire tasted out in the fresh air, washed down with hot cocoa, as the sun rose over the lake. *Bracing* was the word he used; it was new to me and so I wrote it down in a little book I kept for brand new words—Dad's idea.

At home, I didn't have to share my father with anyone other than my mother. And yet sometimes I longed for a brother or a sister, even a twin. I didn't know why exactly, but I was thinking about this as I lay in my hospital bed being pampered by grown-ups. My dad was an only child too, so I asked him, "Did you ever wish you had a brother or a sister?"

He took a long time to answer. I was eating the ice cream Bubbe had sent over and savouring the cool melting chill and sweetness against my raw throat.

"Yes," he said, "often."

"Why did you and Mom have just me?"

He mumbled something I couldn't make out, then added, "Miri Monks, it just turned out that way."

I was in the hospital for ten days, the longest in my life with the exception of my recent stay, which is what made me think about this first time. As soon as I got home, I wanted to see Bubbe. I was on my way out the front door when my parents called me into the kitchen and sat me down. They almost never did this unless something terrible had happened.

"Bubbe Zelda's gone," Dad said.

"Gone *where?*"

My dad pulled me into his lap. He was a tall, lanky man with beautiful, expressive hands that looked sculpted by Michelangelo, and he wrapped his long arms around my waist. "Bubbe came down with the flu. It progressed to pneumonia and a secondary infection we couldn't treat. The antibiotics didn't do much; the bug was resistant."

I was too stunned to think. I knew Bubbe had gotten her flu shot, but Dad said the doctors got it wrong that year. A bunch of questions flooded my mind. *When did she get sick? Why didn't anyone tell me? Did she catch it from me? Was she in the same hospital at the same time?*

For as long as I could remember, I visited Bubbe nearly every day after school and we sat at her kitchen table with sweet milky tea and her homemade apricot *rugelach*, as I told her my news. Bubbe Zelda was a glamorous older woman, full-figured and graceful, impeccably dressed, always with a string of pearls and matching earrings and bracelet, not to mention a slash of crimson lipstick. Once when a snotty friend asked her if her pearls were real, she paused dramatically, thumped her ample bosom and quipped, *"I'm* real."

She had such cool things in her old Upper West Side apartment, like a giant box of buttons more precious to me than coins or jewels, which I loved to sort through and make up games with, as well as a collection of dozens of purses hanging on hooks like puppets, which she let me borrow for dress up and impromptu one-girl stage plays. Bubbe Zelda liked detail, lots of details about my school days and my life in general. If I didn't have a good story, I'd make one up. The week I got sick, we'd seen each other every single day because the weekend was spent celebrating her seventieth as a family. Bubbe doted on me and pampered me with gifts and kisses and hugs, and I sometimes found her staring at me when she didn't think I was looking. I knew I was Bubbe's favourite person, and she was my second favourite, after Dad.

Dad was the reason I decided to become a doctor—a psychiatrist, in particular.

As we're Jewish, the prayers, rituals, and burial happened fast. I don't remember the funeral all that well after these many years, only my parents' big bust-up beforehand about whether I should be allowed to attend. My father was opposed, whereas my mother felt I should have the chance to mourn Bubbe and to learn about death; I was old enough, she insisted. Mom won, as usual, and I needed to be there.

After the funeral, we drove to the graveside at Mount Hebron Cemetery in Queens, a sweeping burial ground spread out as far as the eye could see. The day was very cold but with a crisp shining sun that made everything shimmer and look like it had been outlined in black ink. The cruel brightness made my head and heart ache. I'd never been to a cemetery before, and the expanse of graves that went on and on, the outcropping of headstones, reminded me of unending fields like the ones I'd seen on a cross-country trip through Iowa. But these were fields of dead people. Thousands of them, each with loved ones left behind.

We drove to the area where Bubbe was to be buried, and there was a huge open hole—the casket had already been lowered before we arrived—and some burly men who were not part of the family standing around with shovels. I stared down into the hole; Bubbe's white pine casket was pale against the dark wound of earth. We stood in a semi-circle as Rabbi Stein distributed black ribbons to our family. Dad helped me pin mine to my winter coat—which was bright red, my favourite colour at the time—and I watched as Rabbi Stein nicked the grosgrain with a small knife to make a tear, a symbol of the tear in our hearts, he explained.

There were about a dozen of us at the burial ground, though the synagogue had been crowded with many times that number at the funeral. I did remember a big crowd there.

Rabbi Stein began a prayer: "*Barukh atah Adonai Elohenu melekh ha'olam, dayan haEmet.* Praised are you, Adonai our God, Ruler of the Universe, the true judge.*"

He talked on, but looking down at the casket, I didn't believe Bubbe Zelda was inside. Or she was trapped, alive and still breathing. I had to know for sure. Panicked, I ran to the hole, sat down on my bottom, and slid fast down into the ditch. The smell was musty, rich, an inside-of-the-earth smell, an inside-of-the-body smell, and I was within all of it now. I heard the group of mourners gasp, my mother cry out. And then my dad was talking softly to me, stooping low and reaching for me. But I was down too far, about six feet under, and I was crying and shaking, still coughing a little.

"We need to open the box!"

I was standing on Bubbe's white pine casket; there was no other place for my feet.

My father shucked off his winter coat, murmuring reassurances to me, as he lay on his stomach, his arms extending down into the pit. I raised mine, and he managed to grasp me under my arms. Dad got into a crouch, and with help from the other men, he lifted me out, as if I were just being delivered, born out of the very earth.

I was wet and filthy, covered in mud and leaves, as cries shook my body. "Where's Bubbe? Where is she?"

My father swept both arms around me, encircling and confining me, his suit jacket streaked with damp earth. Rabbi Stein came over to me and put his hands on either side of my filthy head, which was clotted with clumps of earth. He looked straight into my eyes. "Your dear Bubbe Zelda has passed," he said in a low voice, "but her *neshama* is here with us. Her essence, her love. Now, her *neshama* is on its way to Heaven, to the eternal world. It will leave her body once it is buried in the earth, like a beautiful bird flies into the sky."

Rabbi Stein led us through more of the prayers and then asked each of us to share a thought, a wish, a memory, or a feeling about Bubbe. I couldn't believe that she was inside that box, and I was terrified that indeed she was and needed to be freed. Nothing made sense. I felt she was somewhere I could find her. I was going to talk to Bubbe Zelda and would eat her *rugelach*. That's what I said. Some relatives laughed, and I coughed—I still had a bit of bronchitis, a remnant of my flu.

My father spoke last, his voice and hands trembling. He addressed Bubbe directly, as if she were still alive and he was talking to her. I believed he was. He said, "Ima, forgive me."

Though I had only half-listened to my mother and other relatives and close friends, I didn't want to miss a word of what my father had to say. It was a key not only to aspects of Bubbe I didn't know or understand, but to my father's heart.

"Ima, I forgive you. I forgive you everything. You were all I had after Dad died when I was seven. Ima, forgive me."

His words puzzled me. I didn't know why he had to forgive Bubbe and why he asked Bubbe to forgive him.

After Dad spoke, he alarmed me by emptying the first fistful of earth onto Bubbe's grave. It made a gritty clattering sound in the quiet winter morning. Seeing or sensing my distress, Rabbi Stein approached me once more and murmured, "Miri, this is how we show our love. This is our tradition, our final ritual act, honouring your Bubbe. We bury our dead in the ground so they can return to the earth. Ashes to ashes, dust to dust."

My mother's hand clawed, gouging earth; straight backed, she walked to the edge of the pit, opened her palm to the sky, and let the rich brown dirt sprinkle through her spread fingers onto Bubbe's casket. We each took a turn, and I filled both hands with earth and slowly opened them, watching the dirt splay against Bubbe's coffin. I felt as if I had drifted outside of my body and was split in two—spectral, a stranger to myself, floating free. But with this falling earth, I would reach her, my Bubbe, my Bubbe Zelda.

My father and a few of my uncles each took a turn with a shovel, heaping earth onto the coffin until it was completely covered. Then the workmen took over until the hole was filled.

Where is she now? Is she still somewhere? What is her body like now that she no longer breathes or thinks or feels or has a heartbeat? Where is her soul? Has it flown to Heaven, like a bird soaring high in the sky, as Rabbi Stein insisted? Can I believe that?

My dad was crying, and I went to put my arms around him; I had never seen him shed tears before. "Miri Monks, find a stone. Find a beautiful stone for Bubbe's grave. We put a stone."

I didn't want to let him go, but I set about looking for a beautiful rock, sifting through the dirt. It was hard to find a stone, a good one. There were lots of pebbles and gravel and sand, but finding a pretty stone was hard and gave me momentary respite from my confused and painful thoughts. At one point, my mother tried to pull me up from under my arms, but I made myself limp and went right back to my foraging. Frustrated, I stood up to find my father, but saw that he was not among the knot of mourners at Bubbe's grave. Everyone was talking and sharing memories, so I slipped away and wandered among the gravestones looking for my dad.

It took me a while to find him. At last I spotted him sitting on the cold, damp ground in front of a small gravestone of pink granite. (A year later, we would unveil a larger stone of the same beautiful rose-coloured rock mottled with silver and onyx for Bubbe.) Dad's long arms were wrapped around himself, as if to keep warm.

I looked at the engraving on the stone, *Miriam Gildener*, and felt my bones lurch. No one ever called me Miriam, and yet the name was on all of my official forms for school, emblazoned on my birth certificate.

"She only liked to be called Miriam. Three years old going on sixteen," Dad said softly. "We did everything together. I taught her the alphabet and the sounds of each letter and read to her every night before bed. We had a language of made-up words, just us two. *Deetoe* was thank you, and *Shadah* meant do it for me, whatever needed doing. She liked me to sit on the edge of her bed until she fell asleep. She wouldn't accept anyone else, not even our mom or dad. She would cry and call out for me until I came and sat. I waited for the sound of her slow, steady breathing. I loved that sound."

"But that's what you do for me. Every night."

"That's right, Miri Monks."

"I thought it was *only* me."

My father went quiet for a while. Then he said, "Miriam would have been reading by her fourth birthday. Just like you were."

I looked at the tiny, perfect pink, black, and quartz marbled stone. There was my name and the dates *1938–1941*.

"When I was five years old, I came down with measles," my father went on. "Miriam caught it from me. When I heard from my parents that she had died, I wished it had been me. She died, I lived."

My father, agile and lean, lifted himself from the ground without uncrossing his legs, pulled a lovely black stone veined with mica from his pocket, and placed it on his baby sister's grave.

"Your Bubbe tried to forgive me. But she couldn't. She could not forgive. Ever."

I wanted to comfort my dear father, to comfort myself. There was a stone bench beside the grave, and Dad sat down and pulled me into his lap. I sat there for a while until he lifted me to standing and then stood up himself, brushing off his coat and pants. Not long after, I returned home with my parents. But I was not the same girl I had been before. Forever changed, changed forever.

It took me years to understand all of what had happened on that day and in my father's past, which was carried inevitably into my present and future as surely as donated blood passes from the giver's vein into the person who receives the infusion. I now have two children of my own. I vowed when I became a mother that I would not keep secrets from them, secrets that could fester or explode, and yet I do. I am.

I've begun to read up on Mount Hebron Cemetery where my family is buried and how it entwines with Bubbe's history. I am trying to decide if I want to be buried there, if I want to be buried at all.

Bubbe was an immigrant from Minsk and came to this country as a child of eight, my age when she died. She and her family lived in an apartment on the Lower East Side, which only housed immigrants from her village in the old country. They formed an informal society that provided social life, a synagogue, health coverage of a sort, and burial benefits. Bubbe's community purchased the tract of land at Mount Hebron where most of my family are buried. There is a gate at the entrance of Bubbe's family plot with the name of our family and their original village in Minsk. I barely noticed it on the day we buried her.

I understand that we keep secrets from our children as much to protect ourselves as to protect them. I've forgiven Bubbe. I've even forgiven my father. I will hold my secret only so long as I can still forgive myself.

I've begun to collect stones. I store them in clear glass jars, and they are placed here and there around my apartment on Tupper Street in Montreal. They comfort me and bridge the past, present, and my future. We place stones on the graves of our dead to honour them. Stones speak to the dead. Stones testify to the presence of life. At least for the moment.

THE
ARRANGEMENT

Guy

Fact or Myth: *In fertile cervical liquid, sperm can live for up to five days.*

Natalie and Rachel huddled together doing their happy dance, splashing strangers as they sang "Ring Around the Rosie," as if they were kids, while I leaned against the edge of the rooftop heated pool, watching steam rise into the snowy Montreal evening.

"I have this feeling it stuck," said Rachel, her voice wild, jubilant. "This time we nailed it."

Nailed it? Didn't like that verb.

"You would know," Natalie murmured.

"I want this for you," Rachel said. She finger-combed her wet-slick hair straight back from her forehead. "For us."

Natalie nodded and hugged Rachel while I felt increasingly superfluous, though I was enjoying this hot steamy pool on a cold winter's night, our treat for Natalie's birthday. I lifted my arm out of the water and felt a refreshing mentholated sensation as my hot, wet skin met the chilly air.

Sad, purposeful sex had taken its toll on us, as had the battery of fertility tests and procedures. We went through the grief of three successive miscarriages and the terror of an ectopic pregnancy. Natalie nearly died. She had so much scar tissue in her uterus that she couldn't carry a child to term. I hoped a baby would heal us, bring us back together. I couldn't imagine my life without Natalie, my childhood sweetheart, *l'amour de ma vie*. My life didn't make sense without her. And it would be great for Rachel, Nat's best friend from way back when, who always said she wanted to experience pregnancy and childbirth but didn't have a loving partner.

A few months ago, we had sat in our cramped living room, considering options. I opened a bottle of Bulleit and poured a glass for each of us as Rachel flipped through a booklet Natalie had picked up at her ob-gyn's office, reading aloud facts and myths about conception, pregnancy, and childbirth in a wry tone.

"Let's try it at least," Natalie said.

To be honest, I was uncomfortable with her plan. It was all too *Handmaid's Tale* for me. I didn't want to hurt or betray Natalie. You'd think that she would have been threatened, but Natalie and Rachel are—*were*—like sisters, and this broader definition of family suited them. I grew up with a Catholic mother who didn't believe in birth control and a mostly absent dad who still managed to father seven kids. We weren't a model for the health and stability of the traditional nuclear family. I threw out the suggestion of egg donation, and Natalie dismissed it with a wave of her hand. Too clinical. We'd had enough of that to last a lifetime.

Fact or Myth: *Women ovulate on day fourteen of their cycle.*

The first time, we met up at our house, in our bed. The sex was silent and mechanical, a military operation, and I deployed. Natalie was kind of off to the side in a strange crouch during the whole business, which made me feel bad, as if this big idea was a big mistake. And Rachel lay there on her back, rigid, eyes closed, a human sacrifice. I felt myself float out of my body, watching, as if observing another man. It was an eerie, uncomfortable feeling. One that came back, years later, after my trucking accident.

The three of us rendezvoused a couple times after that, always at our house, in our bed. Disaster. After each encounter we sat in the living room, drinking bourbon, getting smashed, hoping our awkward shame would dissipate in relation to how much alcohol we consumed.

Part of the problem was that I had a crush on Rachel. I didn't let myself dwell on it too much. I'm good at blocking out what I don't want to think about, but sometimes I needed to daydream, like you need a drink or a cigarette or a chocolate bar. It was purely chemical, the way I felt my heart beat faster when she was around, and I got clumsy and inarticulate.

Natalie and Rachel were physical opposites. Natalie was short and solidly built with strong shapely legs. She had wide-spaced, expressive brown eyes and smooth olive skin, while Rachel was willowy with secret curves that she camouflaged in loose clothing. Her hair was auburn and her eyes a colour I had not seen before, a kind of amber that sparked golden when she was happy, startled, or angry—a flash of sun through lightning—intermittent, dangerous, brilliant. She talked with her hands, making shapes in the air. And then there was her personality. Deeply kind. And game.

We were about to give up on our arrangement when we planned the birthday weekend at the Bonaventure Hotel downtown. It was a big splurge for us since making ends meet was a continual challenge. But what is life without a splurge now and then?

Fact or Myth: *Having sex daily increases the chance of conceiving.*

Things just felt different that winter weekend at the hotel. There was something about being in our own city but away from the daily grind, plus the luxury of room service, the novelty of the rooftop heated pool, and the small tablets of expensive chocolate on our pillow. The whole experience was new to the three of us, like time out from time.

We made love, we fucked, we shagged multiple times over the weekend, and I would have, could have done more. Back then, I was pretty keyed up and tightly wound sexually. Hell, I was young and horny. So were the women.

We had sex in the bed with its fresh sheets and fluffy cream-coloured duvet, we fucked on the floor, and—I should be more embarrassed to confess—we got it on in that rooftop pool, which was more challenging physically than I'd anticipated. (There was a window of time when we were the only folks in there and no lifeguard to bust us.) I just felt free, released, delivered (excuse the pun), and so did Natalie and Rachel. A flow state that's impossible to force or will—it just happens and what bliss. I never thought I'd be comfortable in a threesome, but it felt just right that weekend. Making love to Rachel and Natalie and Natalie and Rachel making love to me and to each other. All this love all around. Yeah.

Fact or Myth: *To conceive a boy, have sex right before ovulation. Want a girl? Do it several days before.*

Rachel was right. Natalie was with her when she did the home pregnancy test and it turned positive and then went with Rachel to the gynecologist for a more official physical exam and blood test.

I was teaching music at Royal Vale High School in NDG and planning a coffee house evening where the kids would perform and we'd serve light snacks to the parents. The coffee house prep meant long days and evenings. I loved that job; it was what I was meant to do. The news that Rachel was pregnant with my child—I mean ours—came to me belatedly. Still, I was thrilled.

Once we knew Rachel was pregnant, we met and agreed that we wanted to name the baby after Natalie's father, a firefighter and all-around great guy whom we were all very close to growing up. He was a kid at heart and joined in our games, coached our teams, and ferried our band with all of its gear to gigs around Montreal. We were set on Jean-François for a boy and Jeanne-Françoise if we had a girl.

Still, Natalie and I had been through too much trauma to celebrate. We were anxious up until the end of the first trimester and cautiously optimistic after that. Funny, how Rachel's pregnancy drew me closer to Natalie. I was grateful.

Rachel gave us a blow-by-blow account of all of her food cravings and aversions, her heartburn and urinary urgency, her low backache and acne, her need to buy a new bra every few months as her breasts grew to unforeseen proportions, her difficulty finding a comfortable position to fall asleep and her trouble getting up, as well as her newfound pleasure in midday naps. She had leg cramps and pink toothbrush, brainfog and swelling of her ankles and feet. She complained to Natalie within my hearing of her vaginal discharge, enough each day to soak her panties. Oh, and did I mention hemorrhoids?

Frankly, I think Rachel enjoyed being pregnant but didn't want to make Natalie feel like she was missing out. Natalie had loved expecting, that sense of being special, of possibility, of feeling like a sacred vessel—until it all went wrong every time. I couldn't help the thought that it was my fault. The guilt didn't help.

Rachel was sexy when she was pregnant. No surprise there. The ripeness was enticing—the dewy glow to her skin, despite a few blotches here and there, the lush, ample breasts. I tried not to think too much about my attraction, but my dreams ignored my will, as they will, and there we made love often and passionately the bigger she became and came and came and came.

Fact or Myth: *Fetal movement can occur anywhere between the fourteenth and the twenty-sixth week, but generally closer to the eighteenth to the twenty-second week.*

Rachel appeared at our apartment late one night more excited than I'd ever seen her. She was around six months pregnant. She'd felt the baby move and wanted us to feel it too. Taking turns, we put our palms, then our ears on her swollen belly. Natalie didn't pick up anything at first, but I did—a sharp kick or pummel.

"What's it like, Rach?" Natalie wanted to know.

"Well…." Rachel lay down on the floor on her back, feet spread wide, something she'd been doing more and more these days to counter backache and leg cramps. "It's like a fluttering, a butterfly in my tummy, a bubble bursting, being turned upside down at an amusement park."

"But I felt a real hard kick," I said. "Nothing fluttery about it."

"So do we want to know if it's a boy or a girl?" Rachel asked.

"Yes," Natalie said, "so I can shop for the baby."

"Shit, Nat. We're not going to colour-code my baby."

The *my* caught us all up short.

We managed to free our schedules to attend the next ultrasound screening, a late afternoon appointment, the final one of the day.

"What is *that?*" Natalie asked pointing to the screen.

Our obstetrician, Sarah Bloom, a tiny, waiflike creature who was disconcertingly young, smiled like the sun coming out from clouds. "That's your baby's penis. Clear as day."

Fact or Myth: *Starve yourself, starve your baby.*

We headed out to the all-night diner in Saint-Henri, The Star, later that evening. Rachel, slim to start with, had been advised by Dr. Bloom to gain twenty-five to thirty-five pounds and was already past forty, going strong. She claimed one side of the booth, and Natalie and I sat together opposite her. Rachel ordered steak and eggs, hash browns, toast with peanut butter, a side of pickles, and chamomile tea. We watched as she spread her toast with peanut butter and studded it with sliced pickle. Natalie and I had plenty of coffee, plus a fruit salad and cottage cheese for her and a giant corn muffin—the size of a baby's head, I might add—for me.

"So we're decided on names, right?" I asked.

Natalie and Rachel nodded. "I'm happy with Jean-François," Natalie said.

"Yeah," Rachel added. "We can call him JF, same as your dad."

We were all quiet for a bit, remembering Natalie's dad.

Rachel took a long slug (that's the only word for it), draining her tea, and motioned to the waitress for a refill of boiling water. "But there's things we need to talk about," she said, taking a big bite out of the peanut butter pickle toast. "What are we going to tell him about his parents?" This came out garbled, her mouth slightly cemented with peanut butter, but we got the gist.

"Well," Natalie said, "maybe we don't have to tell him *anything*."

"The thing is," I pointed out, "he'll know who his birth mother is, Nat. It's all in black and white."

"Didn't know that was a thing, kids checking out their birth certificates," she snapped, picking up her coffee with a violence that sloshed it over the cup onto her shirt. "Shit!"

I dabbed at her with the paper napkin, spreading the stain, leaving little white clots on her blouse.

"Quit it, Guy!" Natalie said, pouring the spilled coffee from her saucer back into the cup. "He'll assume I'm his birth mother. We'll be raising him."

Rachel polished off her toast, glugging down a full glass of water. "Well, maybe we could kind of divvy up parenting. He could stay with me sometimes. We're all three his parents, right? Would give you guys a break. It's no picnic, parenting, from what I've heard. Especially in the beginning."

Rachel called the waitress back over and ordered dessert. Natalie and I shook our heads but asked for coffee refills. I had the feeling I'd be up all night anyway and had an early start to school. I'd crash after.

We sat there and talked and talked until way past midnight about our dreams and wishes for our baby boy, our dreams and wishes for ourselves as parents. Most of our ideas were vague and pastel, oddly familiar from images on TV and in movies. I had a nagging thought at the moment, and it became more pronounced later: *we don't have a clue, not one of us.* Yet, it was a coming back together for the three of us; we were reminded of how much we loved each other.

"Maybe we don't need to lay down the logistics in stone," I said. "Take it as it comes."

Natalie did an odd thing, her head circling between a yes and a no. Then she got up from the table and squeezed beside Rachel, who was tucking into her apple pie à la mode.

"Hey, sweetie," Nat said, "can I have a bite of that?"

Rachel smiled. "Get your own, sister." But then she filled a spoon with steaming pie and ice cream and fed it to Natalie.

Fact or Myth: *Real labour has probably not begun if contractions are not regular and don't increase in frequency or severity.*

On a sweltering August afternoon, I was teaching a group of pre-teens a new song on guitar at the local YMCA day camp when I got the call from Natalie. Rachel was in labour. Or thought she was. Rachel was forty weeks; it was time. Natalie was heading out to Rachel's apartment, which wasn't far from ours, and told me I should come over after work. Then she added, "No rush."

When I got there, I was surprised to see that Rachel, who had been exhausted and irritable, barely able to waddle, had a surge of energy and was mopping her kitchen floor and cleaning out the cabinets and fridge. She was huge, but still carrying mostly in front, a gain of fifty-one pounds, she'd boasted to us.

"So far it's just like period cramps!" she chirped. "I'm okay! You can go home, Guy."

But I stayed. I helped clean and organize Rachel's apartment and packed her hospital bag, following orders from her and Natalie: a plastic rolling pin for counter massage, warm socks (her feet were always cold), a hairbrush, a bottle of champagne labelled with Rachel's name, sugarless lollipops to keep her mouth moist, a robe and PJs, a toothbrush and toothpaste, heavy-duty sanitary pads, a travel Scrabble set, packs of raisins and nuts, a going-home onesie for JF, a receiving blanket, and an outfit for Rachel of light loose sweatpants and cotton tee. Done and done.

A few hours later, I ran out to get a late dinner for the three of us and when I returned, Rachel's contractions had intensified considerably. She paced around and kneeled on the rug, leaning over a big armchair. Natalie filled the bathtub and helped Rachel in and out and in and out.

"You hungry?" I called out to the two of them, not sure what to do or how to help.

"Fuck off, Guy!" Rachel snapped, and I felt as if I'd been slapped across the face.

Natalie gave me a sweet, knowing look. I mouthed, *should I?*, pointing toward the door. She shrugged. "Take a walk, but keep your phone on."

"Course."

I ambled around the neighbourhood for several hours. The night had cooled, and there was a luscious breeze through the trees that swept against my sweaty neck and back, refreshing me. I savoured this time alone—soon it would be rare, Natalie and I devising ways so that we each could have time to ourselves, spelling each other in the rondo of rocking and feeding and changing. Lights glowed in windows, and I wondered about the people inside their houses, couples and families and singles. I thought about what they were doing while I was walking around, waiting to be called back in.

I was thinking about how much time and energy we'd put into getting pregnant. It was an all-consuming goal that blocked out everything else, even what it would be like to have a child, to be parents. We hadn't given that much thought. Enough, that is.

Being one of seven, four boys and three girls, and the baby in my family, I hadn't had experience caring for infants or small children, though my older sisters had plenty of practice changing diapers and feeding and calming me and my brothers. Sure, I had my fantasies about teaching JF to play guitar, jamming with him, maybe even coaching his band, chauffeuring them to gigs as his namesake had, but these dreams leap-frogged over infancy and toddlerhood. *Would I, could I, be a good dad?*

Roaming around the neighbourhood, I realized how famished I was, that I hadn't eaten since lunch. Though some take-out rice and souvlaki was sitting on Rachel's counter, I didn't feel ready to go back there and headed to the Star instead. I ordered a big breakfast of eggs, toast, sausage, and home fries, plying myself with cup after cup of coffee. The coffee was really good there, strong and always fresh with a nutty flavour. As I ate, I remembered our talk a few months back. We still hadn't come to a firm decision about the parenting arrangements. Or about when we would tell JF who his biological mother was.

Rachel's idea of sharing parenting seemed like a pretty good plan to me. There were some unconventional families at my school, in the neighbourhood. And they weren't even considered so unusual these days. We should do what was best for JF. Still, as I polished off my breakfast, I had the niggling feeling that Natalie wasn't quite comfortable with this set-up, even with telling our son that she wasn't his biological mother.

As I paid my bill, I got a text from Natalie to get back to Rachel's place. When I arrived, Rachel was sitting upright on the floor, leaning against Natalie's chest with Natalie's arms around her. Rachel's eyes were squeezed shut, and she grimaced and rocked with each contraction. Natalie rubbed Rachel's neck and shoulders, applying a cool cloth to her dripping forehead.

"Now," Natalie would say each time Rachel had a contraction. I started timing them as they got progressively more intense and closely spaced throughout the night. At around six o'clock in the morning, Rachel rocked forward to kneeling and gasped, as clear fluid gushed from her and pooled on the floor. Her contractions were coming five minutes apart by then, and we helped her into our van and headed to the hospital.

Fact or Myth: *Childbirth is divided into three stages. The whole process averages about fourteen hours for first-time mothers.*

We saw no sign of Dr. Bloom when we got to the hospital, but a nurse took us to the birthing room. Natalie helped Rachel change into a hospital gown, and then the nurse gave both me and Natalie sterile scrubs to put on over our clothes, while she checked on Rachel and the fetal heartbeat.

Rachel was now in what I'd learned was transition, the most painful and demanding stage of labour. Her contractions were less than two minutes apart, lasting a minute or a minute-and-a-half with intense peaks that I imagined like breakers in the sea, one after another after another with little space between.

Rachel grunted involuntarily in pain and vomited, her body sweating and shivering at once. She'd decided against pain relief but screamed that she'd changed her mind.

At that moment, Dr. Bloom wafted in. I was standing by Rachel's shoulder, and Natalie was on her other side. She examined Rachel, and we could both see her smile that lovely smile of hers. "Rachel, your cervix is fully dilated. You can push!"

Natalie helped Rachel into a pushing position, semi-sitting up, and the nurse coached Rachel on when to push and when to pant or blow. As we'd learned in our delivery classes, I tried to be helpful, comforting, supporting her back, holding her hand, but she snarled, "Don't."

Instead, I fed Rachel ice chips while Natalie helped her relax between contractions, applying a cool cloth to her neck, shoulders, and upper back.

"Feel," Dr. Bloom said, guiding Rachel's hand to the baby's head, which was just beginning to crown, and then he slithered out into Dr. Bloom's arms. "Here he is!" she said. "Your beautiful boy."

And Rachel crowed, "I'm not pregnant anymore!"

Fact or Myth: *A newborn is as round and smooth as a Botticelli cherub.*

Our son, JF, announced his arrival by peeing in a golden arc and screaming until his tiny face turned purple. He weighed nine pounds and four ounces, and he was twenty-three inches long with a head circumference of fourteen inches—a pointed head, I might add, from his struggle into the light. I was terrified to hold him and was stiff and awkward. Rachel and Natalie were impatient with me, but our nice nurse took the time to help me get comfortable with my new son.

Rachel decided, last minute, to breastfeed and because it was beneficial for the baby's immune system, Natalie supported her decision and helped her to get the baby latched on.

My terror came back when I was driving the three of us home from the hospital with our bruiser of a newborn in his new car seat. I took it slowly and cautiously, and got us back to our house in one piece.

Rachel moved in with us for a while, the four of us together in our cramped little house. I found once I got more comfortable with JF, I was okay with getting up at night to change his diaper, walk him up and down the block to ease his colic, and just hold him. I loved when he clenched my index finger in his tiny starfish-shaped hand and felt a tenderness I'd never experienced before.

Fact or Myth: *Having a child brings parents closer.*

At two months, when JF looked up at me and broke out into a wide-open loopy grin, I felt that everything was right in my world. A couple months later, I watched him, a proud papa, as he boxed up on hands and knees and tried to crawl, again and again and again, finally succeeding—backwards!

Rachel was still breastfeeding, but at five months her milk supply was inadequate for JF and she had intense inflammation in her right breast, as well as a lump. She figured she had a blocked milk duct and went to see Dr. Bloom.

Dr. Bloom said it didn't present as a blocked milk duct and referred her for a mammogram and ultrasound. The lump was biopsied, and Rachel was diagnosed with Stage 2 breast cancer.

Apparently, pregnancy and the huge influx of hormones flooding Rachel's system had acted like jet fuel, triggering and quickening the growth of cancer. She moved back to her own apartment for her treatment, and Natalie went with her to help out, bringing JF with her.

Natalie nursed her best friend and also took care of the baby. I helped out as much as I could, taking JF to our place and looking after him when Natalie accompanied Rachel to all of her treatment appointments. I was getting more comfortable being a dad.

We celebrated JF's first birthday party at Rachel's apartment, where he toddled over to me for the first time. Afterwards, while Rachel was cleaning up with JF soldered to her hip, Natalie told me that she needed to talk.

"I don't know if this will come as a surprise," she started.

"What?" I couldn't think.

"We've fallen in love."

It came as a shock and yet wasn't a surprise at all, simply inevitable. I shook my head and laughed low in my throat.

"So you think it's funny?" Natalie said, flashing her dark eyes at me.

"I was just remembering our talks about custody and when we would tell JF who his parents are, who his biological mother is."

"So?"

"Won't be an issue now."

"Right."

So JF grew up with two mothers that he adored and a father who came in and out of his life, alighting here and there. If I could go back and do it all over again, I would. I wish I could. He thought of his parents as his two mommies and me as a kind of uncle. When he was two and I came to pick him up for an outing to the zoo, he looked up at me and asked, "Are you my daddy?"

DEVOTION

Delia

On a wintry Friday in February, Delia's husband Joshua idled
the van, backing up traffic, as she stepped out into a snowbank
beside the Physio-Sports Centre. Regaining her balance, Delia lifted
her palm, fingers stiff, and Joshua pulled alongside her, wheels
sputtering snow.

Delia sensed his reluctance to leave her, but whisked him away,
fingers loose.

Joshua moved in slow motion as Delia briskly entered the clean
white lobby with its pool-blue lettering, waiting and watching for
her husband to fishtail away into the confusion of beeping cars. She
lingered, then went outside again and walked at a clip to a dingy
brick building a block and a half away, entered the shabby lobby,
and rang for apartment 3.

Elijah always took forever to come to the door, and Delia
wondered what he was doing inside. At last, he buzzed her in, and
Delia entered his apartment/studio, which felt like an oasis.

Delia relished the graceful order here, as her shambling Victorian
house with Joshua was overrun with clutter. In truth, she and Joshua
were the proverbial "odd couple," and the charm of their respective
styles had worn off. Director at a community centre for abused and
homeless women, Delia functioned best in an orderly environment,
while Joshua, a pianist, composer, and music professor, exploded
into whatever space he occupied, plunking down coats, keys, and
puddles of sundries. Their older home was always in the midst

of fix-up or repair; stray parts lay strewn about for weeks, often months, while Joshua lost essentials: his phone, notes for a lecture, even his wedding band. All this chaos was a vortex that threatened to suck Delia in, a painful reminder of her schizophrenic brother, Jake, not to mention the non sequiturs and weird comments their teenage daughter Morgan was prone to making lately, as well as her move down to the basement, worrying Delia that all the pot Morgan was smoking was making her see things that were not there and hear voices inside her head, but their most annoying problem lately was Joshua's insistence on talks about what was *going on*, and all of this verbiage—nearly emetic—churned out more of the clutter Delia was drowning in within her marriage.

Entering Elijah's studio, Delia felt a fluttering of anxiety, but emptied her mind. She had two hours of not having to talk and to listen to only what was necessary. And then the tranquil bus ride home alone.

Elijah never greeted her with the perennial *how are you?* What a relief, what a terrible question. He simply swept his arm in a graceful motion that might have been an invitation to dance, that said, *you're here now, let's get started.*

Delia savoured the look and feel of the bands, balls, and bars Elijah whipped out like toy surprises in candy colours. She began with the pink bands, doing the exercises prescribed to heal her frozen shoulder. She'd never heard of this ailment until her own right shoulder congealed; its pain and her limited range of motion made it tough for her to fasten her bra, do her swimming workout, or get a proper night's sleep. Elijah was methodical and patient, correcting Delia's form with a gentle but firm touch.

What serendipity that she'd met him! It had been back in November following an appointment at the Physio-Sports Centre. The place was an aquarium—injured souls on view—as they sweated and struggled with the challenge of healing. After a few perfunctory questions, Delia's therapist strapped her into a fearsome, pulsating machine and promptly forgot about her. She extricated herself from straps and buckles and fled to the local dépanneur in search of

Advil, cheap wine, a case of beer, and every lurid tabloid she could lay her hands on to get through another bad night.

At the cash, Delia couldn't retrieve the wallet she carried in her back pocket without burning shards of pain flashing through her shoulder and radiating down her arm to her wrist and fingertips. She cursed. With a groan, she managed to yank out the wallet and pay for her armamentarium of anesthetics, all the while feeling some guy's dark shining eyes on her.

"Are you all right?" His voice was lilting, his phrasing formal.

"Not exactly."

They moved to an empty aisle, and he extended his arms, palms facing each other.

"Put your hands inside mine," he directed in a soft, deep voice with an enveloping lilt that sounded Middle Eastern.

She obeyed.

"Can you push against my hands?"

She could.

Without questioning who he was, Delia let him run her through a few more manoeuvres. Something about him won her trust—or was it simply desperation? "Have you had an X-ray of your shoulder?"

She nodded.

"The neck as well?"

"They couldn't find anything."

"Did you have an injury, a strain?"

"It came on slowly last summer. A heaviness in my shoulder and arm. Not being able to unhook—well, you know—get out my wallet, pain during the night, difficulty sleeping."

"I suspect you have adhesive capsulitis. Frozen shoulder is the lay term."

Just to have a name for her problem filled Delia with unreasoning joy. No matter that the diagnosis was armchair-style, in a Côte-des-Neiges dépanneur. She had frozen shoulder! Adhesive capsulitis! Delia wanted to shout it out to the world.

The stranger introduced himself and explained that he was a physical therapist. The card he handed her was adorned with six sets of varying initials, and he told her that he had been trained at Harvard. His company was called HOPE, an acronym for Healthy Options and Performance Excellence. Ordinarily Delia would have scoffed at this cheesy phrase, but chronic pain, or perhaps Elijah's fateful appearance, drew out an earnest streak.

Delia set up her first appointment. She'd been seeing him twice weekly ever since.

A mirror lined one wall of Elijah's studio, but it made Delia self-conscious; it was enough to have his eyes on her.

This frozen shoulder thing had really gotten Delia down until she found Elijah. She was forty years old with a limber, toned body that she'd always taken for granted.

During the pleasant tedium of stretching the pink band the length of the wall, Delia imagined into Elijah, a large blank canvas. *Lives alone, late-thirties.* He stood a few inches shorter than Delia, strong and well-built, on the cusp of stockiness, with dark brown eyes made all the more intense by his shaved head. Delia had no idea where he was from originally, but she suspected Lebanon, or perhaps Jordan. *Wait a minute. Elijah—isn't that a Jewish name? Maybe he's Israeli.* She and Joshua were Jewish, but lapsed of late.

Delia fixed her gaze on the hanging tapestries, one in varying shades of blue and brown, the other mauve and burgundy. "Are these from the Middle East?" She felt silly, even stupid, having uttered that phrase.

"Delia, stay focused. That's it. Keep your elbow in at your waist. Good."

She continued, waiting.

He sighed, smiling with his eyes. "They're from one of the Persian carpet places on Laurier, near Parc. Okay?"

Finally, her hour of exercises was over and she could prepare for her massage. When Elijah returned, she was on her stomach on the massage table, slipped between cool sheets. His hands were cold at first, and that initial touch was bracing after the achy warmth of the exercises. Elijah began at her neck and worked slowly, deeply, methodically on her upper back, shoulder, arm, and hand. She'd never had a massage quite like this, as Elijah didn't lift his fingers from her skin until the treatment was over. Even when she turned, his hand holding the sheet as a drape, he kept his other hand on her shoulder and commenced again. There were moments of such exquisite pain, Delia felt an urge to bite down on wood. Instead, she breathed in rhythm with Elijah's coaching and found her way through. Other moments were deeply relaxing, and by the end of the hour, she was transported to another place, not sleeping, but in such a state of loosening that she took a while to come to, saliva pooling on the white sheet.

Each visit was a new miracle.

Early in March, after her usual charade with Joshua, Delia rang and rang Elijah's buzzer, but he failed to appear. This had never happened before; Elijah was steady, Delia counted on that. Then she spotted a small note that had fallen to the floor. *Back in five minutes,* Elijah had scrawled.

Delia waited for him, five minutes, then ten. Anxious, she dashed into the street, pacing the aptly named Côte-des-Neiges neighbourhood. A new blizzard had blanketed the city the night before, and the streets and footpaths were obscured by layers of white, grey, and black ice. Cars were buried, and trees and houses glimmered iridescent in children's cut-out shapes. About five blocks from Elijah's studio, Delia spotted him helping a woman along the hazardous paths. Delia recognized her right away as Lola Mathews, a large lady in her early fifties who'd had a hip replacement and several knee surgeries, not to mention a neck injury that often required a brace. In spite of her bulk, Lola favoured pastel track suits in Easter egg hues with matching crocheted hats. She had prominent teeth and long hair in a mesh of colours that she wore loose and wild, like its own ecosystem. No one would ever guess that Lola was Katie's mom. Katie was a star: tall, willowy, and classically beautiful, though careless about her appearance as if it were an encumbrance. Katie was brilliant, excelling in science.

Lola had her appointment before Delia, and they often greeted each other coming and going. Delia knew her from their kids' school and from volunteer work. Both Delia and Lola gave time to the Cove, a halfway house for the mentally ill. Lola led the painting workshop, and Delia the word processing seminar. Lola had been volunteering at the Cove for over a decade, Delia just a few months, when they met. Most of the participants had schizophrenia, an illness Delia and Lola were all too familiar with; Lola's mother had suffered from the disease, as had Delia's beloved brother Jake. In fact, Delia was meaning to ask Lola for coffee so she could talk through her worries about her daughter Morgan and pick Lola's brain about what she should do before things got out of control. They were both mothers of teenagers, after all.

When she was growing up, Delia's parents had travelled frequently, leaving her and Jake on their own, inseparable, a family unit. When at nineteen Jake started hearing the jeering voices—when he could no longer sculpt the pieces he made from junk metal, when he writhed awake at night—he took his own life, leaping off the roof of Dawson College. Delia was fifteen.

Though Jake had died years ago, Delia still suffered moments when she was hollowed out by grief.

Once, Delia asked Elijah something about Lola and he answered simply, "A great lady."

"I know her from the Cove; we volunteer together."

"Lola does a good deal of charity work," Elijah went on, "though she wouldn't use that word. She devotes herself."

Elijah's words burrowed in. Lola always had a sweet smile on her face that was so genuine it put Delia to shame. Clearly it was a struggle for her to walk, to do anything and everything, yet she was still smiling, pleasant.

Sweating as she struggled through drifts, Delia kept Lola and Elijah in her sights. They neared a place in the sidewalk so occluded by snow that it was more of a crevice; pedestrians could make way in one direction only. If someone was in a hurry, they'd have to venture into three-foot drifts to get past. In this narrow space,

Elijah swung Lola ahead of him as if she were a sylph, his hands on her shoulders to guide her.

Delia saw a group of teenage boys clot impatiently behind Lola and Elijah. The leader of the pack waited a moment, then yelled out, "Move it!" Delia struggled closer, moving into the road to pass the knot of pedestrians.

"Get going, fat bitch! Both of you grunters."

People got ugly in Montreal during the six-month winter, a kind of mass seasonal affective disorder that made a lie of the truism that Canadians were polite. In disgust, the animal and his pack shoved past the couple, roughly jostling Elijah, and tromped into the street.

There was Lola's white van, a beached whale in the snow, shrouded with the past week's dumping, now downy white, ice crusts and grey sludge beneath. Lola clicked open the rear hatch, and Elijah found scrapers and set to work clearing her windshield and windows.

Delia was close enough to hear them now, standing at the edge of the street between parked cars, but they didn't notice her. Lola was saying that she'd baked Elijah cookies, his favourite, a whole tin.

"That's all I need, Lolly."

Lolly, this was new. Elijah had no moniker for Delia, and she felt a stab of envy.

"The almond crescents," Lola went on, "with marzipan and jam filling."

"You're bad, Lolly. You're partly responsible for this." He patted his barrel chest and paunch, which strained the seams of his jacket.

Lola retrieved a large colourful tin from the open hatchback while Elijah replaced the snow scrapers and slammed the trunk closed. Standing behind the car, Lola presented Elijah with the tin, which he managed to hold under one arm. He began to use the other to gently, almost tenderly, help Lola to the driver's side and into her car, but she shooed him away.

"You're always telling me to be independent!"

Elijah shook his head, smiling, retreating to the snowy sidewalk, both arms now wrapped around the cookie tin. They both watched

Lola open the driver's side door with aching slowness, as she prepared to move her considerable bulk into the seat.

Without warning, a sapphire-coloured SUV bombed through, hitting Lola from behind and propelling her several yards into the street. Elijah dropped the tin, its cover came off, winter wind sailing the lid like a Frisbee, the almond crescents scattering. All was chaos.

Delia called 911 on her cell. Elijah was on the ground, administering CPR to Lola. The police arrived with sirens and flashing lights and cordoned off the area; EMS came next.

Emergency medical technicians carefully lifted Lola onto a stretcher. Delia saw her blood in the snow—drops, ribbons, and seeping pools of scarlet in the winter palette of grey, black, and white. Her body appeared inert, her face an unearthly whitish blue, that crazy hair, the most real part of her, like a living creature.

Once they had safely loaded Lola into the ambulance, Delia heard Elijah speaking to the rescue workers in French, and a moment later, he slid into the ambulance as well. Delia hailed a cab and followed them to the Jewish General Hospital. She found the floor, the waiting room, and Elijah in one of the orange plastic chairs, head in his hands. Delia sat beside him, both watching and waiting.

Elijah looked up for a moment, surprised to see her there, then turned distractedly and murmured, "I have a number for Lola's daughter." He fumbled about but couldn't find his phone.

"Take mine…. But I don't have her number. I could call my daughter, Morgan. She might know. She and Katie are in class together."

"I think I remember it." He stared at Delia's phone, as if it were a conundrum he needed to solve, then tapped out the numbers.

Heads turned to look at him, stirred from the unbearable state of watching and waiting.

"Hello, Katie. This is Elijah Zahreh, your mother's physiotherapist. There's been an accident. Please get to The Jewish as soon as you can." Then he gave Katie the wing and the floor.

Elijah seemed uncertain of what else to say and signed off with a shrug.

"I hate to give alarming news over the phone, but did I indicate the urgency?"

Delia's skin warmed. "You did."

She had no idea of the time or how long they'd been waiting; outside the grimy window, dusk and snow blued with twilight.

At last a man in a white coat appeared. He looked around, then a nurse pointed him in Delia and Elijah's direction.

"Are you the family of Lola Mathews?" he asked.

Delia glanced at Elijah, and to her surprise, he nodded. They stood, and Delia closed ranks with Elijah, a shield.

"I'm Dr. Lessard. Please come with me," he directed. Delia followed, and no one paid any mind; they might have been brother and sister. "I'm terribly sorry," Dr. Lessard said. "We lost her. She had multiple injuries from the impact and lost a good deal of blood." He looked at Elijah. "Your mother was a tough lady, but she was not an entirely well woman."

Delia's eyes expanded.

"She experienced emboli in several end-circulation areas—that is, areas of the body that have no redundant blood supply—her brain, heart, lungs."

The doctor went on with his clinical speech, though he didn't seem like a bad sort. Delia noticed his kind hazel eyes, the surprise of trembling hands as he spoke.

Delia took Elijah by the arm. He seemed sapped of all of his bulk and strength, fragile.

"I should have helped her into her car," he said. "That was what I wanted to do."

Delia led Elijah out of the hospital and into the street. The wind was strong and wild, a keening, almost human. Delia had to cover her mouth to catch a breath. The cold was terrible, it burned. Delia led Elijah into the warmth of one of the many cafés on Côte-des-Neiges and went up to the counter to order lattes. In the quiet settling between them, Delia listened to the *tacka-tacka* of ice pellets against the café window.

Outside, they made slow progress through the crevasse that stood in for a sidewalk, uneven and slippery, even under the heavy tread of winter boots. People nudged past them. Everyone was in a hurry, such a hurry—but to where, and for what? Delia pulled out ahead of Elijah and they threaded along in single file, uncertain where to go, what to do. The absurd image of a cyclist pedaling through and around snowdrifts arrested her attention; insane winter construction forced them into the street.

"I have to go back to my studio," Elijah murmured, his voice flat, nearly toneless. "Clients."

Delia felt an urgency to stay with him, a private and bewildering need. "My pink scarf—I left it at your studio," she found herself babbling. "And my travel mug—I'm sure it's there too. I'll go with you."

Outside Elijah's studio, an elderly man was waiting in a long duster coat, his back bent like a question mark. Elijah put both arms around his shoulders in a protective arc. "Morris, I'm sorry, I've had an emergency. We need to reschedule. I will call you tonight, okay?"

Morris glared at Delia out of the tops of his eyes like a boxer, and she cringed.

Elijah turned him around. "Where is your car? I'll walk you." He turned to Delia and threw her a ring of keys. "Go inside and warm up."

She caught the jingling bundle in two hands, her face flushed, avoiding Morris's stink eye. Entering Elijah's studio, Delia caught sight of her fuchsia scarf and her travel mug, which he'd placed on a chair near the entry. These alien objects stood out amid the peaceful order of his flat like gaudy ornaments.

Delia entered Elijah's kitchen, opened his cupboards and fridge. He had so much food. There were fresh fruits in jewel colours and plump healthy vegetables, butter in a crystal dish, and a dozen large eggs.

She would cook them breakfast; breakfast in the evening would be a comfort, sustaining. Delia prepared their meal with an absorption that gave her mind a respite.

"Well," Elijah said, as he rejoined her in the kitchen, a sweet, surprised smile on his face, "you've been busy. Lola was like—well, she meant a good deal to me."

Delia poured coffee into their mugs and spooned up fluffy mounds of eggs. "Everyone loved her at The Cove. I don't know what they'll do without her."

Elijah looked down at his steaming food, his head in his hands, just as he'd sat at the hospital. Then he shook his head. "Lola was something."

"Please," said Delia, "while it's hot."

"Did you check your messages?" Elijah asked, beginning to sip his coffee and eat his eggs.

The question punctured her pure peace for a moment, and she shook her head, reaching for her cell, then checking her purse. "I think you have my phone."

Elijah reached into his pockets, checked his coat, then knocked his head roughly with a palm. "Delia, I'm sorry. I left it at the hospital. I think I did, anyway."

Delia's anxiety quickened. What if Morgan was trying to reach her? Well, she could always contact her dad.

They ate in silence for a while, and Delia took pleasure not only in the food, but in looking after Elijah for a change. Just as she was putting up seconds on toast, his phone rang and he got up, wiping his mouth. "I should get this."

Delia moved about the kitchen quietly, listening. "Yes, she's here," she heard Elijah say. "There was an emergency. No, no, she's fine, yes, of course. I managed to lose her mobile; it's a long story really. Let me give her to you. Delia can explain."

Delia felt her voice freeze in her throat, but she shook her head and mouthed, *I'll call him back,* and heard Elijah say, "She'll get back to you. Thanks, Joshua."

Elijah sat back down again, but Delia could not think, move, or speak.

When he saw her expression, Elijah got up and put his arms around her. "We're both in shock. You forgot to call Joshua; he must have been sick with worry. Here, sit." He lowered her back into her chair. "I'm sure he'll understand," Elijah said, "once he hears what happened. He is a very empathetic man... and he's crazy about you."

Delia felt her eyes burn.

"I've gotten to know him a bit," Elijah said. "He always calls after your sessions to get an update. I keep him posted on your progress. In a month or two, you won't need *me* anymore."

Delia excused herself and retreated to his bathroom. She ran the tap hard, pure glacial cold, and splashed her face and neck, now hot with tears. After a while she came back into the room and Elijah said, "You've been crying."

She nodded.

"I wish I could cry."

"Who was Lola to you?" she asked, as they moved into his small living room and settled on the couch. She pulled a pillow into her lap and clutched it.

"What? I don't know. We had a strong connection."

"That hair of hers, Elijah, it gave off a smell."

"Like a pine forest. I loved Lola's hair."

"I never told Joshua I was seeing you."

Elijah chuckled, a low secretive sound that unnerved her. "He always knew—we run into each other at the gym. I didn't realize I was your secret."

Delia's face warmed. "Joshua deceived me," Delia said.

Elijah nodded slowly. "Only out of devotion."

She let that sink in and settle like a stone at the bottom of a pond.

"I'm going back to the hospital to meet Lola's daughter, Katie."

"Can I come with you?"

"Delia, you should go home."

Delia walked the entire way home through billowing clouds of blowing snow, like crystal smoke, a brilliant sun shining through iridescent shards. She walked and walked until she was wet, exhausted, nearly numb. Joshua opened the door to their home and folded her into his arms. He kissed the top of her head, her cheeks, and then her cold, damp lips, as if bringing her back to life again.

"I know, I—let me."

"Shhhh."

She wanted to ask him about Morgan. Was she home? Was their daughter okay? And then she heard Morgan jogging down to her basement bedroom, her feet thudding hard like rumbling thunder.

Joshua shepherded Delia into the house and helped her peel off her wet things. She kept waiting for him to say that they should talk, but he didn't, and she understood that this time they wouldn't have to do the post-mortem.

Soaking in the tub, so hot she could barely stand it, Delia shut her eyes and wondered about the day, as she listened to the comforting sound of the kettle whistling and Joshua padding about the house, his footsteps a disembodied presence.

WILL THE
WORLD PAUSE
for ME?

Morgan

Vibration before sound, that's how it starts. You could be at home, school, anytime, anywhere. You hear mumbling and feel your lips twitch as you mouth words. Keep on your noise-cancelling earphones, never go anywhere without them. Listen to The Weeknd on continuous loop, *I would die for you*, sing along with him.

You are alone.

In the zone.

Just know.

Beneath, around his voice are other voices talking just to you. They whisper, then hiss. *You will die for you, you will die, yeah, baby, yeah.* Don't listen. They crank up the volume and play tricks until you can't hear The Weeknd, only horns beeping, children whispering and weeping.

Morgan.

The name sounds strange in your own ears. They have gouged it from this world, cut it out of the language with a knife.

The voices start soft, secretive.

Morgan.

Remember who you are. You be you.

You're failing several courses in grade eleven, too much flooding through eyes, ears, nose, mouth, every pore, so you can't take in what your teachers are saying. Take math.

Open your textbook and read.

Make connections between numeric, graphical, and algebraic representations of quadratic relations and use the connections to solve problems.

Construct tables of values and graph quadratic relations arising from real-world applications (e.g., dropping a ball from a given height). Sight might fright.

Black words, white space blinds. Check the signs.

You snap the textbook shut and see every grain and scratch in its cover, get lost in the pattern you slattern for who knows how long. Wrong song.

Soon school's out for summer and maybe you'll be well. Drawing like mad, he he. Making comics not sad. You've started a graphic memoir, a day in the life sort of thing. If you can hold out till summer, you and Collier can work on it together, build a whole world around you. Around you two, like animals in the zoo.

You hide what you hear and see. Me. Give over the fucking key!

Delia and Joshua ask about your day, well, what can you say? Mom hugs you and it's electroshock. Mind her frozen shoulder! See how you hurt her, can't help but hurt. Stay pert. Wear a skirt in colours that make sounds.

Rainbow is swishing sweeping swelling. Yellow is beep, beep. Blue, waves rolling in, crashing tin. Red, a scream, which is why they call it bloodcurdling. Mom's voice silvery, Dad's a rock—hard, geologic.

Put your hand in the socket.

Sleep is out of the question. Doll's severed head, red glowing eyes. Nightlight. Pure fright.

Time is the abyss, sad, weary, leery.

Who said that? All teary.

You hear a black feral cat, skinny, yowling, like an ambulance coming. That's something. There are more wild stray cats in a pack, pack-cats. With rats. *Tat-a-tat.*

Inside or out? Outside in.

Woo to their side, the dark ride. Against the tide.

We've got you, Morgan. Listen! And you will survive.

Strain to block them, closing ears, eyes. They threaten and terrorize.

We will turn your vagina black, prick your eyes with a tack.

Text Collier from the washroom, then go outside for a cig. Worst day. Ever. Never. Your mind's going. Gone.

It's happening. Again.

Meet me out front.

Cunt, cunt, cunt.

"Coll!" You rejoice when you see them and stuff your earphones into your backpack. They are worthless today. No way.

"Thoughts out loud, too many thoughts." Being born, it hurt to come into the light.

Coll's eyes look scared for you. "We'll walk it off."

They are the only one you can trust. Must.

You head to the Lachine Canal, the day so hot the sun is alive and will peel off your skin and scorch your heart.

At last you're alongside the water and you can feel a breeze off its churning surface. Collier sweeps their arm around you, their touch different from anyone else's. It calms you—a little. You glance over, see a feral cat on their left shoulder, its eyes gem green.

"Coll, that black cat on your shoulder! Do you see it too?"

They tap both shoulders, shrug, then shake their head no. So. *So?*

When the light hits the cat's eyes, they glimmer like emeralds. It yowls at you.

"Coll, hear that?"

The cat leaps onto Collier's other shoulder, the right. Sight. Bright. Tight. Light. Kite. Bite.

"My mom pretends she's a bird," Coll says. "A wild, weird, scavenging bird, picking at garbage. She likes being this bird. Morgs, I told you about that, it got inside your head."

Maybe Aurora put the feral cat in your head as torture. Collier's mother never liked you. Jealous. Zealous. Perilous. Your cats will eat up her bird. Aurora absurd.

You pass by the sculpture garden. Families together, gathering to barbecue, kids kicking a ball, and you know you are outside of all normal life on this radiant spring day with the buttery sun and cerulean sky.

It's a lie.

You like the sound of that word, cerulean. Keep it in your head.

Doll's head, math book, doll's book, math's head. Dead, dead, dead.

Tony, Katie, Penny, Louise. All a tease. Doll's alive, against you. Tony Katie Penny Louise.

"Everyone's trash-talking me. See?"

Collier pulls you in close to their chest.

Wind picks up off the water, sun hides behind puffy clouds. Noise in your head, too loud. The earth laid waste. Take a taste. Fear makes you ill. Till?

"C'mon Mor, let's break into a clip."

You reach the rocky beach, and your whole being is filled with loveliness and light shot through skin blood bones. You shine bright.

Wild wind and sun that beats down in waves like the water washing toward shore. Feel it in your core.

Naked, shimmy down rocks into the canal and gasp from clean cold water. Scratch thighs that sting. What you see and hear and know it will ring.

Collier splashes you, water ices cheeks, burns eyes, spurts up your nose. Freezing toes. You splash Collier back and water fight. Clear blue sky of the mind and warm dazzling sunlight.

Stay in the water a second, a minute, an hour. Shivering, climb up those sharp rocks. Collier gives you a hand and your socks. Scramble into clothes, drag on wet, clammy skin gritty with sand. How you love them. Can they save you? Bring you back to the quiet of before. When you were free and had choices.

Now, where are the voices?

TRACKS

JF

When I was a teenager, I was in love with a girl called Morgan Rosenblum. Our gang had a clubhouse on the Lachine Canal—a battered old bright orange container that was never used or carted away—and we hung out there after school and on weekends, the place to be.

Morgan's sixteenth birthday party was in June and Montreal was beginning to get warm at last. Nine of us arrived early to set up. We had loads of munchies, plenty of beer and wine and weed, but it was bigshot me who brought the supply of Oxy. I had access through my dad, Guy, who used the pills for pain relief after his near-fatal trucking accident. There were stashes here and there in his apartment, and I stocked up, cagey, little by little, until I had a whole mess of them.

The party was the night I was going to get next to Morgan. I had friends, but she barely noticed me unless she needed help in math or science—maybe because I wasn't artsy enough. At first, I hated that she called me Jean-François because no one else did, but later I liked that she used my formal name. She was the only person who chose to, and I saw it as a sign signifying, well, something.

Morgan was a talented artist who drew cartoon stories, and hers were in colour, all the bright yummy hues of hard candies. Because of Morgan, I immersed myself in graphic novels, which I'd known nothing about. I heard her mention Art Spiegelman and Alison Bechdel, Aislin and Jillian Tamaki, and I immediately got ahold of their books so I'd have conversation-starters. Morgan loved Indian food, which I'd never tasted, but when my dad was trying too hard and planned an evening out for the two of us I told him I wanted to go to an Indian place, Darbar, Morgan's favourite.

I thought long and hard about what to get Morgan for her sweet sixteen and decided on a set of drawing pens I'd overheard her talking about with Collier, her best friend. I saved for weeks and made a trip downtown to DeSerres to buy them and couldn't wait to surprise her at the party.

In short order, bottles of red and white wine were poured and beers popped open. Louise brought some Maker's Mark that went around our circle and kicked off a lifelong love of bourbon and its smoky warmth.

Tony, who played five instruments and had his own band, was in charge of the music; Collier put out gummy bears; and Morgan lit a joint and passed it around. Penny had baked a lemon-filled cake for Morgan with indigo blue icing—Morgan's favourite colour—and soon everyone was high, attacking the chips and peanut M&M's, the gummies, and the licorice Twizzlers as the munchies set in.

"Ready for birthday cake?" Penny asked, a friendly redhead who got us all involved in a weekly game night like a bunch of seniors, and who took great trouble to hide her ample breasts and belly under baggy tops.

"Tributes!" Collier said. "Tributes first! Let's start with why we love the lady of the hour."

"Me first," said Penny, tugging her sweatshirt. "Morgan, I love you because you're fucking kick-ass. You remind me never to take any shit from *anybody*. Still working on it."

The group cheered, and when the hubbub quieted, Tony spoke up. "You're hot, Morgan. You're fucking hot."

"Oh, shut up, dick," Collier hissed.

"Well, it's true," chimed in Louise, looking around at the rest of us from behind her thick black-framed glasses. "Morgan is a hot beverage, to quote Starbucks."

"You're incredible, the most talented person I know," said Katie, the brightest girl in our class, the best in science. Since her mom, Lola, had died she had lived with her grandmother and spent all of her vacations in St. John's, Newfoundland, where her dad lived and worked as an oceanographer. "I would trade both feet for *half* your talent," Katie added, pulling back her hair and twisting it up on top of her head, her long, willowy arms bare and graceful in a white tank top. Funny that Katie would envy Morgan, as Katie went on decades later to become a noted conservationist working in Costa Rica to save the sea turtles, famous enough that I read about her in the paper. Back then, she was a buddy and we often talked science.

Morgan leaned in and kissed Katie on the mouth to hoots and hollers.

"You saved my life," Collier said. "Again. I'm a cat with nine. And lots of near misses."

Collier was born a boy, but when I knew them in high school, Collier was "fluid." Fluid was milk and orange juice, not people, and Collier's fluidity made most of the boys and mean girls go off. Thank God they had Morgan. The two of them went way back.

I was kind of marginal myself. My grades were too good, for one thing, and I had two moms. Didn't see much of my dad.

Everyone was quiet after Collier spoke up. Of course, Collier had to be at the party, but except for Morgan, none of us were really close to them. Collier earned my respect for being who they were, despite the fact that it caused them mostly grief.

I watched Morgan kiss Collier, a long deep dance of lips and tongues and mouths that radiated through their bodies and into ours. We all got lost in it, and I wondered if I had it wrong about the two of them being just friends. The others must have been having similar thoughts because no one hooted, hollered, or cheered them on. We just went quiet.

When they drew apart, I drank Morgan in. She had a startling beauty, not a classic or conventional type of look. She was a tall, curvy girl with athletic shoulders and thick dark hair that flowed all the way down to the small of her back. Her skin was a creamy olive, and her eyes, almond-shaped and heavy-lashed, were a pale seafoam green that took you by surprise because you expected them to be brown. Her lips were full, and she had a strong prominent nose, which only added to the character of her face. I had overheard her talking one day in the hall with Collier: "I love my big schnoz," she'd said, "it's the only thing I got from my dad."

I would've liked to hear more of their conversation, but Collier shot me a look, pure poison.

The tributes to Morgan went on. When my turn came, I kept it simple. "I love you, Morgan." I was too drunk and high to worry and the words tumbled out.

She looked at me for a brief moment with those pale green eyes, then tilted her head back as Collier cooed, "Aww."

Penny lit sixteen candles on the blue cake, then one more for luck, and Morgan covered her eyes like a little girl before making her wish. Collier's eyes were shut at the same time, wishing right along with her. I wish I knew her wish; I could only imagine. And what did I imagine? I know now what I wished I had wished for her. And for myself.

Most of us had brought gifts. I didn't see Collier give her anything, but I expect they did so in private.

Penny gave her a giant white vibrator called the Magic Wand. "You will never need man, woman, or anyone in between—again." Katie presented Morgan with a package of vintage issues of *Raw*, and Tony, a year's supply of Dentyne Fire, her favourite gum. Now it was my turn. I handed her the package I'd carefully wrapped in shiny midnight blue paper and silver ribbon. When she opened it, Morgan sighed and touched her heart. She came over and held my face between both hands and gave me butterfly kisses on my cheeks, lips, eyes and neck. I didn't want the moment to end.

The dancing started after midnight. I passed around the Oxy, feeling pretty full of myself, and swallowed mine fast without thinking, watching as my more experienced friends crushed and bit and chewed the pills to get the biggest buzz. I was feeling no pain, but the effects weren't as intense as I'd expected or hoped. Morgan and Collier got up to dance and everyone fell away to the sidelines to watch the two of them move together. They danced down to the floor, and their heads swivelled and bounced, their arms undulating like plants beneath the sea. And then as Percy Sledge's "When a Man Loves a Woman" came on, they slow danced, holding each other, Morgan dipping and Collier dancing up into her, bending deeply at the knee so one lanky leg was between hers to be closer still. Morgan and Collier. *How could I have missed this?*

After a while, Morgan slipped outside—I had these antennae so I always knew where she was without having to look. Everyone else was still dancing like crazy. All at once, there was a deafening beat on the ceiling of the container and I heard Collier shout out something I couldn't make out.

I rushed outside with a few of the others. There was Morgan atop the container, dancing up there, drunk and high and wild. Others crushed out of the clubhouse as Collier tried to soothe Morgan, to talk her down, literally and figuratively. Who knows what she was seeing and hearing and feeling?

I later learned that Morgan, even cold sober, saw things that were not there, but hid it from everyone except for Collier. She also heard voices speaking inside her head. That explained the earphones she rarely took off—they helped drown out the internal noise.

I came to understand a bit of that noise myself, later on.

Tony and I boosted Collier up on top of the container. Once on the roof, they put both of their arms around Morgan, enveloping her as she cried and laughed and laughed and cried, something I'd seen Collier doing too. We could hear the murmur of Collier's voice and the painful cries of hers.

Collier crouched behind Morgan and hooked their arms beneath her knees, helping her scooch her bum to the edge of the container. When she let go, a net of arms and hands were ready to break her fall and get her back inside.

We barely had time to breathe a collective sigh of relief because not long after, a crew of boys a year or two older than us showed up at the party and crowded into our clubhouse. Word had gotten out. After they'd helped themselves to our provisions, their leader Luke insisted we play Truth or Dare. Everyone was game except for Collier.

"Not playing," Collier said.

"Then piss off," Luke ordered.

"Not going anywhere," Collier sing-songed.

"Come on, Coll," urged Morgan. "Don't be a party pooper."

Collier shook their head, long platinum hair swinging around their pale, thin face.

"Bro, if you aren't playing, you need to fuck off."

"Don't call me bro."

Luke gave Collier a dismissive shrug and muttered under his breath, "Freak."

More beers, wine, and bourbon were passed around. Luke had brought weed, boasting that it was laced with cocaine, and a second batch mixed with LSD. As he handed around a rainbow joint, a light rain began to fall on the roof with a soothing sound that reminded me of the ocean, which I'd only visited once in my entire life on a summer break with my moms in PEI.

People settled into a circle along the edges of the space, Luke and Collier on either side of Morgan with me opposite her. The game started with Louise. She asked Tony, "Truth or dare?"

"Truth." He slugged down his beer.

"What do you hate about yourself?"

Everybody laughed, though it wasn't a funny question.

"I'm a shitty musician."

"No way," said Penny. "No truth there."

Tony turned to Louise. "Truth or dare?"

"Dare."

"Kiss Collier in their most private place."

The pronoun was considerate, the dare cruel.

"Collier's observing," said Morgan, pulling them into her hip so the two of them were sitting as close as possible.

But before things could escalate, Louise leaned over and kissed Collier lightly on the forehead. It was a great move—Collier's brain, thoughts, their most private place. Even Collier smiled, a sad, secret smile.

Everyone looked at Collier, waiting.

"Okay. Morgan, truth or dare?"

"Truth."

I looked at Collier, and we both felt a rush of relief because they would never dare her to do anything humiliating or dangerous.

"Who's the love of your life?"

"*Tu es l'amour de ma vie.*"

"Shit," said Katie. "Tell us something we don't already know."

The game went on and on deep into the night, going around the circle many times.

Luke turned to Morgan. "Truth or dare?"

"Dare," she said.

"I dare you, beautiful, to let me make you feel better than you ever knew you could. Or should."

"Fucking poet and doesn't know it," Collier murmured.

It was quiet; the rain had stopped. Then everything moved too fast. Luke hustled Morgan outside while three of his friends held Collier down.

Some of us tried to free Collier. In a druggy, delayed reaction, the rest of us surged out of the container, looking for Morgan, so we could stop Luke from whatever he was doing to her. We searched the canal, ducking into other containers and old, stranded train cars, but there was no sign of either of them anywhere. In desperation, we ran up and down the tracks. Still no luck.

Finally, Katie called 911.

I dream of that night, again and again. Sometimes I'm the rat, squeaking as it feasts on crumbs and ash caught in spills of blood-red wine and stinking beer. Other nights I'm the police, arriving at the wrecked bright orange container, empty of kids, smelling of booze and sweat and weed. Some nights I'm Morgan, terrified, unsure what is inside and what is outside, wishing the voices inside my head would shut the hell up. Other nights I'm Collier, loving

Morgan as I already do, knowing that I couldn't save or protect her, as hard as it was to save and protect myself, having to live with that—or deciding not to—wondering if I could go on in this world that is cruel and ugly with few glimmers of light.

It was close to dawn when the police found Morgan alone in an abandoned shoe factory along the canal near the town of Lachine. She was not breathing, and medics rushed her to the hospital where she was pronounced dead.

The cause of death was opioid overdose. There was evidence of sexual intercourse, though no one will ever know if it was consensual.

We all went to the funeral, and then there was a small memorial service for her closest friends that Collier organized. Somehow I got invited.

It was cold and bright on the afternoon of the service with a sharp wind off the water and the sun gleaming on its surface.

We all gathered on the rocks descending to the waterfront beach on the Lachine Canal, one of her favourite spots, where you could still glimpse the sculpture that looks like upraised flames or hands reaching for the skies. Apparently, it was Morgan and Collier's special place, this beach, and they liked to shimmy down from the rocks and swim in the chilly water, kite surfers in the distance. They are the only two people I've ever known who actually swam in that rocky, restless part of Lake Saint-Louis.

We each had a chance to share a memory of Morgan. And then while her mom held the oak urn, one by one we reached in for a handful of her ashes and tossed them into the foamy water.

Morgan's mother tolerated my presence at the funeral, at the memorial service, but she was cold, dipped in Plexiglas. Her dad simply ignored me. Maybe it had nothing to do with me and my part in Morgan's death, but was simply pure grief. I'll never know.

I intended to go and see them, to ask forgiveness. In fact, I planned it all out in my head and on paper, but by the time I got up my guts to go to their home, I ended up doing something really weird. I later learned that the Rosenblums had split up and that Delia had moved out west. I did write her a letter some years later, but she never answered me.

After Morgan's death, I hid my smarts in high school, though I managed to do all right. I loved biology, anatomy, the details of cells and nerves, tissues and organs. I had a secret dream of becoming a doctor, but I never pursued it. Not because I wasn't bright and tenacious enough, but because deep down inside, I felt rotten to the core, hardly a healer who first and foremost would *do no harm*.

The therapist I saw, an eccentric giant called Nico Tesoro, tried to convince me that what had happened at the party would most likely have happened anyway. The grain of truth in that notion sifted in through my pores little by little.

We had family therapy, and I did group therapy with other fucked-up teens and one-on-one with Nico. Lots of talk and walks, walks and talks. I loved my therapist, who was more off beat than anybody I knew. He helped me. I can admit that now.

I managed to squeak out an acceptance from McGill, but I broke down before beginning my freshman year. Then came time off, years doing odd jobs.

I became a recluse, cut off my family, my friends. I believed I needed all of my time to think, to sort things out. For a few years, I didn't go to school and was out of work. I drifted, stayed in shelters and grabbed meals at food banks. I thought I spotted Luke at the Men's Mission one night, but he was so dishevelled, broken, and dirty, I wasn't sure it was the same guy. Whoever he was, he took no notice of me.

My life was putting one foot in front of the other.

In the book of Numbers, God tells Moses that the Israelites must designate six cities of refuge so that anyone who kills someone by accident can flee there. The murderers will be protected from the wrath of the "blood avenger," a family member of the deceased. The roads were to be well marked, free of obstacles, and wider than regular roads, so that those who have killed someone by accident could go there easily and without delay.

I never found my city of refuge. I remained in place.

I ran into Collier a couple more times—briefly when we were eighteen, and then much later on when we were well into our thirties. I stopped into a café near the McGill campus, and Collier greeted me more warmly than I expected. We sat down for a chat. Collier told me that they had been running the café Isolatoes ever since the original owner, Paulie, had died. Paulie had taken Collier in when they were orphaned and homeless, and had become like a father.

Collier looked well; their platinum hair was twisted up into a bun, and they were decked out in high-waisted jeans; heeled boots; and a billowy, white-ruffled blouse. They no longer sported the ironic smirk that had been like a hand covering their face during the painful years of high school.

We both had the speciality of the house, an Isolatoe, a scrumptious coffee drink with cocoa, coconut milk, Kahlúa syrup, and cream. I needed some sweetness in my life.

Collier filled me in on the past twenty years of their life. They had gotten a degree in set design from Concordia and worked for some years in local theatre. Then when Paulie got sick with kidney cancer, Collier took time off to care for him. After Paulie's death, Collier decided to take over the café. One of Collier's dreams was to host a reading and performance art series at the café, and I could feel their excitement when they talked about it.

Still, we couldn't help but remember that terrible night.

Then Collier said, "I'm thinking of adopting a kid, a girl. I'm making a trip to an orphanage in China this spring with my partner, Cole."

"Wow, that's wonderful," I said. My own life at the time was still stuck and sucked. I liked my work as a biology teacher at Park View High, the same high school I'd attended. I hoped I was "making a difference" and all that, but I was terribly lonely and haunted by ghosts. My penance.

Collier told me that every year they went back to the beach on the Canal and sat for a while honouring Morgan and feeding breadcrumbs to the seagulls, as they'd done together.

"I still talk to Morgan in my head," Collier said. "I dream of her, and she's alive. With me. Again."

We started a tradition that afternoon where I joined Collier at the Lachine Canal beach on the anniversary of Morgan's death and we thought and spoke of her, remembering her life and how it had touched ours. It helped a little.

And that's when a woman came over to our table to talk to Collier, and we all got to chatting. Turns out she was training to be a physician's assistant.

I have Collier to thank for connecting me with the love of my life, only myself to blame that I could not hold on to her. But that's a different story. No, maybe not. Perhaps I just have this one story and that's enough.

MALE *and* FEMALE CREATED HE THEM

Rachel

A glass of cold water washes away the bitter aftertaste of my first few sips of coffee. I used to love coffee—the smell, taste, even the ritual of brewing: grinding fresh beans, heating milk—but ever since chemo, it doesn't taste the same. Yet I feel good to be back on the job. The worst thing about being sick is the outlying sphere you inhabit, losing that sense of who you are and where you belong. I don't recognize my body anymore, and yet I've chosen to keep it as is—no hot, itchy wig that makes strangers more comfortable than it makes me, no reconstruction, no prosthetics. I'm going flat.

Another taste and I look up to see a pale face smushed against the Plexiglas of the staff room, and jump, sloshing coffee on my sleeve. I'm a solitary fish in an aquarium. The kid laughs, dragging white palms over the transparent wall between us.

I plunk down my mug and step into the corridor.

Both of us a gangly five foot eleven, this kid and I stare into each other's eyes. The teenager is slender and sinewy with pale, see-through skin, long platinum hair, and eyes of such a light blue that they look like washed seaglass.

"I'm Rachel Neuman, your recreation therapist."

"Hell help the person who calls me Coll."

"Got it."

"That's just for dead people."

"Sorry?" I run through the information I've just heard in the staff briefing about Collier Sampson: sixteen years old—same age as my son, JF—been in the children's psych ward for over two weeks, non-binary, prefers *they* to *he* or *she*. Doesn't fit in with the other kids, not going with the program, alienated from every*thing* and every*one*.

And then my dark days on this ward come back to me—the hostility of the kids; the infectious sadness; the worry over whether I can do any good, or, at least, do no harm.

I hold out my hand, and Collier takes it in both of theirs, which gives me a little jolt, but I maintain my demeanour. Normally, Collier's gesture would be intimate, or histrionic, and I wonder what they're playing at.

"Got some catching up to do, Collier. See you this afternoon for rec."

Feeling off balance, I head back into the staff room, take out Collier's file, and begin to read.

On my lunch break, I race across the line of buildings that form our new Super Hospital at the Glen site over to the Cedars Cancer Centre. Yes, breast cancer treatment is a triathlon: surgery; chemo; and now radiation, the final push. All free and readily available for someone who has been in dire shape like me.

O Canada!

Swiping my health card, I wait for my name to appear movie-star-like on the big screen and then go back to my treatment room where I greet my technicians, two very young women. I'm forty-two, and these girls don't look any older than my kids on the ward.

Lying down in the twilit room, I settle into the mould they've made of my body and stare up at the glassy ceiling panels illustrating an impossibly blue sky and white puffy clouds, as Sarah Vaughan sings "If You Could See Me Now."

A boisterous laugh escapes me and Melissa and Tam smile. "I know," Tam says. "Sorry."

"No, no, each day something… *unexpected.*"

"When you're ready, put your arms up," Melissa says as Tam slides a support under my knees as if I am getting a massage. "We're going to refresh your marks," Melissa adds.

I raise my arms in surrender and grasp the metal holders as Tam opens my robe, exposing my scarred, breastless chest.

With a pen, Tam marks my body to help position me for the treatment—not only my chest, which is now like a topographical map of a sun-scarred desert—but also along my flanks down to my waist and all the way up to the base of my neck. Melissa reinforces the marks with iodine.

Body as colouring book.

Above my head are the machines, spanking new and white, on long curved stems—one like a giant oculus, the other ones square-screened. They revolve around me like planets around the sun, alchemical flashes zigzagging across their surfaces like green bursts of lightning, and I think, *I'm alive.*

When I get back, Cody is going room to room, rounding up the kids for Jenga. Our chief psychiatrist, Stavros, passes me in the corridor and murmurs, "Niimi meant business this time. Her mom's staying in town, keeping her in ciggies."

We are eight in the rec room including staff.

"I always set up Jenga," says Niimi. "Ask Rachel!"

"How're you doing, Niimi?"

She shrugs, not looking at me, her black hair, slick as licorice, falling about her face while she focuses on stacking the Jenga tower.

All of us on staff are worried about what will happen to Niimi a year and a half from now when she ages out of the children's ward at eighteen. The adult psych ward is hell and we don't have anything better for "young adults" who are really still like teenagers. Niimi has ongoing issues with alcohol, Adderall, Vicodin, OxyContin—

anything she can get her hands on—not to mention her recent suicide attempt.

Donovan bumps the tower Niimi is building, which miraculously remains intact.

"Quit it!" Niimi shouts. "*I'm* setting *up*."

Donovan is one of the oldest kids at seventeen. He beat up his stepfather for punching and kicking his mom, blackening her eye, and breaking her wrist. He's lucky to be here with us instead of in the court system; the placement was due to a diagnosis of bipolar disorder complicated by rage and lack of impulse control.

Donovan won't take no for an answer and joins Niimi, placing three blocks adjacent to one another along their long sides and at right angles to the previous level. Niimi jabs her elbow into his ribs, unfazed by his muscular build and scowling expression, just as Cody says, "Okay, enough guys."

I see a couple of the kids are missing. "I'll make one more round," I tell Cody, get these kids out of their heads for a while. The teens often suffer from obsessive rumination—mind as swamp, thoughts quicksand. I am no stranger to this.

Shoshannah is in her room, staring out the window. I'm struck by how mature she looks for her age; there's something in the world-weary expression of her eyes and her stooped, concave posture, an attempt to hide her full figure. The girl's only fifteen. "Join us for Jenga?"

"What's Jenga?"

"A building game." I'm a fan of Jenga, even outside of work. "A preschooler can play," I explain, "but real skill and strategy are involved, *and* manual dexterity. Each time a player removes a piece and places another on top, the building grows higher yet more unstable—an awful lot like life." My life, lately. I've had quite a few pieces taken away from me, not just my hair and breasts and health. I've lost friends. Good friends, or so I thought. Like my old pal from elementary school, Lisa, who cut me off when I tried to tell her how I was *really* doing to admonish me to *stay positive!* She warned me that my attitude would determine my outcome. Or Constance, who never visited or even called, but sent me an email that read *hoping you're back to normal now.* Hell no, inconstant Constance! There is no normal now, just windows of hope between scans. I must remember there were other people who I never expected anything of who showed up, like Jared, a guy I barely knew from the gym, who just listened and let me vent. He's become one of my closest friends. And of course I have Nat and JF. Why don't I focus on *that* instead of festering about the people who let me down? I'm lost in the labyrinth of hurt and rage some days. Today, for instance.

"Rachel?"

"Sorry, Shoshannah. I was thinking, just thinking." *Here's some obsessive rumination for you.*

"At home, Abba doesn't let me play games. Do I have to?"

"Your choice." Shoshanna was raised in the Satmar sect, I remember from my staff notes, but is eager to get a secular education. She ran away from home, and when her father hunted her down, he admitted her.

Shoshannah goes back to gazing out the window, arms crossed, then joins me. On the way to the rec room, I stop in Collier's doorway. "We're playing Jenga. Like to—?"

"Busy." Collier is slowly and assiduously applying makeup. I have the crazy thought that I'd love Collier to put some good old *maquillage* on me, give me a makeover.

"Okay, we'll catch you later."

About a half hour into the game, after much laughing and kibitzing among the players, Collier appears in the doorway, half-in, half-out, their face a mask of powder, contour, shadow, and brilliant red lipstick. I motion, and they come in, perching on the edge of an empty chair.

Shoshannah looks up. "Are you a boy or a girl?"

I've been asked that quite a bit myself lately. The question jolts like an electric shock. When I look in the mirror naked, I get that same judder.

Collier assesses Shoshannah with pale eyes, roving from the top of her head down to her toes, and then from her toes back up to her head, eyes intrusive as hands.

"Stop staring at me!" Shoshannah squawks, covering her face with her palms.

"See?" Collier's smile is a grimace.

She peers out through spread fingers. "I was just wondering if you were a boy or a girl."

"Shoshannah," I warn, "enough."

Collier watches the game for a while, then joins in. As they slide out a midlevel block, the tower comes crashing down, pieces tumbling onto the table and floor. That's when Collier starts laugh-crying and cry-laughing.

"Hey bro," Donovan says, touching Collier's arm with surprising kindness, "it's okay."

I'm often moved by how the kids connect with each other, their empathy.

With aching slowness, Collier closes heavy-lidded eyes, says, "Don't call me bro," and they start up again, this time just crying.

I am really out of touch, been away far too long.

Donovan holds his large hands up into stop signs and backs out of the rec room, leading the way for the rest of the kids to wander off.

I sit down close to Collier and gently touch their thin shoulder, which makes me think of a bird's wing.

Collier looks up at me with those seaglass eyes. "Are you new? You seem new."

I can't help chuckling. "Old, actually. In terms of this job, anyway. But I've been off the past few months."

"How come?"

"I was sick."

Their eyes expand. "Want to talk about it?" Collier has a slight smile, full lips together.

"Haha."

For a few minutes, their lips make shapes, not sounds, and I wonder what—or who—they hear inside their head. Maybe just their own voice. Talking to oneself is not necessarily a bad thing, or crazy. Trust me, I know.

"Let's check out what's cooking in the kitchen."

Collier unfolds their reed-like frame, and we walk side by side to the kitchen, where delicious buttery orange smells are emanating. "Muffins or maybe cupcakes?" As we peek in, we're enshrouded in steamy sweetness.

"I'm hungry," Collier says. "The meals in here are shit."

I nod toward Lily, who organizes cooking activities for the kids, as she pulls a tray of muffins from the oven. "We'll see if we can taste-test."

Lily hands us each a napkin, then plucks a hot cranberry-orange muffin from the tray, tears off the cap, and hands it to Collier, giving me the bottom half. As we let the treat steam in our palms, visitors trickle in, a flow that will continue during the late afternoon, through supper, and well into the evening.

A stout woman is buzzed into the ward. Dressed in dark, modest attire, head covered with a scarf, and bearing a large carton in both arms, she introduces herself as Sarah Cohen, Shoshannah's mother.

Given the okay, Mrs. Cohen takes the carton of Kosher food back to Shoshannah's room as a rush of other visitors arrive. I recognize Niimi's mother, Koko, from the last hospitalization. She looks more like a sister than a mom. It's not only her youthful attire of leggings and sweater, but her fairly unlined skin and glossy black hair, just like Niimi's. She had Niimi as a teenager, so she *is* young.

Koko's brought cigarettes, and Cody gives her and Niimi a pass to go out on a fifteen-minute break in the fresh air. As they head out to the elevator, Niimi glances my way, taps her heart with a bunched fist, then chants something under her breath. I try not to show my disapproval about the cigarettes. My philosophy is that life will fuck you over on its own without you helping it along the way.

Another woman comes in as they go out. Her face is haggard and bruised, framed by sawed-off bleached blonde hair, and she is dressed haphazardly in a patched flannel shirt and torn corduroys that hang off her thin frame. Her left wrist is in a cast. She holds a brown paper sack in her trembling right hand, its top rolled down, and introduces herself as Maureen, Donovan Walsh's mother. I ask for the sack, unroll it, and see it is filled with socks of every colour, texture, and weight. Here on the psych ward, we have our own version of "The Things They Carried," like in that classic Tim O'Brien story where each soldier keeps a talisman to help get him through the Vietnam War. These kids have their own private wars, their own special things.

I too need a talisman.

I spot Collier pacing the corridor, lurking in doorways and listening in, lips working, as Donovan shouts, "Can we have some privacy, man!"

"Don't call me man," Collier snaps back as I rush over to head off the conflict.

"Hey Collier," I say, my hand on their shoulder, steering them out of Donovan's doorway, "I'm going to set up tomorrow's activity. Give me a hand?"

"Why would I want a visitor in *here*?"

"I know our policy is frustrating: no friends or lovers, at least right away."

They make a little wiggle of shoulders, then hips. "Well, let me count my friends *and* lovers. And we can't have our own *phones*. It's medieval!" Collier covers their face with long pale fingers, head shaking with disdain.

"So you're going to help me, eh?"

"More Jenga?"

"No. C'mon, I'll show you."

Collier pauses, hand on bony hip, then walks beside me down to the rec room voguing like the street models in *Paris Is Burning*.

My cancer recurrence was spotted eleven months ago with an ultrasound early one morning before work—cushiony table, crackling tissue beneath my back, warm gel, smooth glide of the transducer, little beeps like electronic music....

"Ms. Neuman? Ms. Neuman?"

I turned toward the voice; waking was not as easy as sleeping. There'd been some dream and I was trying to catch it like silverfish in an open palm. I can fall asleep anytime, anywhere. It's my gift.

"Easy. Don't want you tumbling off the table. Doctor would like to see you."

"All done?"

"Not quite."

"Bonjour! I'm Dr. Pelletier. I'd like to have a look at you."

She had a lovely, lilting voice, as she took the transducer from the technician and glided it over my left breast. My cancer had been found in the right one the first time, just after JF's birth. "You have many cysts—do they bother you?"

"Yeah, a bit."

As she continued, so did the little beeps. "You have a lot of heterogeneous material in your breasts."

"What does *that* mean?"

"You have busy breasts."

We both laughed. Such a charming phrase, only a Québécois doctor would come up with it. As she slid the transducer up toward my armpit, I felt pressure, a stab of pain, and all at once she turned silent, serious.

"I've been cancer free for years!" I said.

"There is something new, just here. A lesion."

"What do you mean by a lesion? Should I be worried?"

Apparently, yes.

I know I should be grateful that the breast centre fit me in so fast. *I am I am I am.*

My second afternoon back at work, Cody and I gather up the kids for a writing/art project. Each person has their own journal (courtesy of Dollarama), coloured pencils, scraps of many-textured fabrics, glitter, and marking pens. The task is to scrapbook and write about an important milestone or turning point in one's life. The prompt is open-ended so there is plenty of leeway for the imagination, but with a bit of structure. We talk about what we mean by milestones or turning points, or attempt to, before the kids get bolshie.

"This is a jive project," Donovan scowls.

"Milestone? Turning point?" Niimi mocks. "You like your words."

Shoshannah runs her fingers through the pots of glitter and fabrics, lifting up one marking pen and then another. "It's too personal. Why would I get into all of this with *you*?"

Collier seems like they're in a trance, a somnambulist, following Shoshannah's lead by touching everything, putting glitter in with the fabrics, interleaving fabrics with the pens. I feel my face grow hot—don't know if it's anger or a hot flash from the hormone blocker that shuddered me into immediate menopause with all of its accompanying symptoms. I want to say *Hey, it's taken lots of time to pick up all these supplies, to set up the project*, but I rein myself in. "Collier, you want to get started?"

Collier sits down and begins to work while the others linger in a huddle, watching. Then slowly, one by one, they join in, except for Donovan.

I work my way around the table to see how everyone's doing as Cody heads out for his break. The kids are absorbed for about twenty minutes or so when I hear scuffling from the corridor. There is a clomping, like horse hooves, and then an overripe, rank odour so powerful I nearly gag, the scent of something edible and sweet gone to rot.

A woman squeezes sideways into the doorway of the rec room, speaking in a high, shrill voice that does not go with her massive body.

"Where's Molly?"

Everyone except for Collier looks up, too stunned to speak. Collier digs both hands into the green and blue glitter bowls, clawing as if seeking the roots of a tree, their head bowed, eyes squeezed shut. Instinctively, I go around the table and stand protectively behind them.

"Who's in charge here?" the woman demands. "You? Lady!"

"We are in the middle of an activity. Can I help you?" Unfortunately, on the children's ward, visits by family are permitted and the hours are flexible.

"I'm here to take Molly home."

"We don't have a Molly here. Perhaps you are on the wrong ward."

"Come on, Molly!" The woman attempts to squeeze around to the far side of the table, but her girth will not permit passage. Her body odour is more powerful now that she is in the room rather than out in the hallway. She backs out and faces Collier who refuses to open their eyes and look at her.

"Molls! Let's get out of this loony bin. You don't need any more crazy. Jesus, I've spent my whole life running from crazy. We can start fresh; travel the world; eat ice cream and cake for breakfast, lunch, and dinner. Don't believe in school, especially high school. Never learned anything *there*—"

"What is your name?" I ask.

"Louise, but everyone calls me Lou, Lou Sampson. Molly's my niece and I'm her only living relative. She's going to come live with me now and have a normal life."

Normal life. Right.

Collier sinks lower in their seat, face buried in glitter-crusted palms.

"I'm sorry, but you can't take anyone out of the ward. When a child is ready to go home, we have an exit process."

"Well, then, I'm happy to wait." She folds her arms across her shelf-like bosom, plants her feet wide apart, and stands there.

I call Cody, who comes back to the rec room and takes over while I shepherd Collier to safety in the staff room. Glancing at my watch, I see that Stavros should be here any minute, making rounds. He'll evict Louise Sampson.

As soon as I've gotten Collier settled in the staff room with a glass of cold water, Louise flings open the door and heads straight for Collier, reaching out a hand to stroke their cheek. Collier recoils, darting out of reach, and Louise leaves her arm extended in the empty air, the wrist oozing bangles of flesh from a too-tight plastic watch.

"Babygirl, I'm here. It's your Aunt Lou."

Collier curls into a ball.

"We have a waiting area," I say. "The doctor in charge will be here soon. I'll make sure he sees you."

"I don't need a doctor," she declares calmly. "I'm fine, but I could use a glass of water if you would do me that courtesy." She smiles broadly, and I notice that she has surprisingly well cared for teeth, straight and white, and a smile that would be pleasant if she were.

"This is a hospital, Ms. Sampson. There are rules. If you don't obey them, I'll have you escorted out."

"Maybe you don't know the whole story of us. My brother Logan was good with his hands and built Molly a treehouse. When it was finished, Molly's mom, Aurora, climbed in there and set up housekeeping. She refused to come down, but Molly catered to her mom, brought her food and whatever else she asked for. Sometimes, Molly stayed in the treehouse too and that treehouse became their whole world. Both of them suffered from the sads real bad. Molly's mom, Aurora, crazy bitch, jumped. Took her own life."

That well-worn phrase, *took her own life,* got inside my head, and I had the thought that it was not a euphemism: it embodied power, agency and choice, possession and relinquishment, affirmation as well as negation, presence, and absence.

"After he lost Aurora, Logan took off. Molly was shuffled around from one foster family to another. Of course, no need for that. I can take her in, but child services…. She's my girl, right Molly?"

Collier raises their head and stares straight into Louise's eyes, which are so narrow and squinting I can't make out their colour.

"I'm not a girl. I'm not *your* girl. And men are dicks."

Louise lets out a raucous laugh. "I couldn't agree more, Molls. We're both feminists. So tell me, why do you want to be a dick like your dad?"

"I'm not."

"Then what are you?"

Collier's lips curl into a secretive smile while their aquamarine eyes remain grave. "I am."

What I am, I finish silently and feel a rush of blood in my veins making me warm, light-headed.

"Who are you? Tell me who you are," Louise insists.

"Me."

"Molly, stop talking nonsense."

Louise approaches Collier, and before they can get away, she's got her arms beneath Collier's. Just then, Cody appears. Spotting him, Louise drops Collier, who crumples to the floor, knees to chest, head buried in their arms.

Cody has Louise in a grip tight as handcuffs and is hauling her towards the exit. "You need to leave the ward, Ma'am."

"Nature calls. Could you let me use the washroom?"

I call security.

Louise manages to overpower Cody, breaks free, and shuts herself into the washroom in the hallway. Stavros and three guards appear on the ward. They rap on the door, then force it open as Louise bursts out like an earthquake. She is grinning as if she's just won the lottery.

All at once I smell smoke, see red-orange spears of flame. One of the nurses presses the fire alarm while two security guards flank Louise and rush her outside. The third guard grabs the fire extinguisher near the exit and puts out the flames.

The kids are panicked and wild with all the noise, hubbub, and chaos, running this way and that, and Stavros shouts to me to take them outside while building maintenance checks out the ward for safety. It takes most of us on staff to escort the kids to our rooftop terrace.

Once we're on the roof, the kids fan out. The terrace, protected by a high, grilled guardrail, is our sanctuary with its basketball and shuffleboard court, bins filled with balls, Frisbees, and other toys, and a flower and vegetable garden the kids take care of in these brief, warmer months.

Cody starts to organize a game of H-O-R-S-E as Donovan gets shuffleboard going. I look around for Collier, can't find them for a moment, and feel frantic until I spot them in a far corner of the terrace crouched into the protective railing. I go over to them and they are crying and trembling.

Shucking off my fuzzy sweater, I cocoon Collier inside of it until their crying slows and their slender body unfurls like a plant in the sun.

It's twilight, the sky indigo, but there is still enough light to see an aerial view of the city; this day seems both endless and instant. In the corner near Collier, the flower and vegetable garden, which was planted by the staff and the kids on the ward, is just beginning to bud.

"I get beaten up every fucking day," Collier tells me. "The teachers don't do anything."

I nod, listening.

"Girls kick me out of the girls' washroom and boys boot me from the boys'. I piss outside in the trees like a dog."

"It'll get better," I murmur. This was what my dad always said to me growing up when I suffered. They were simple, well-worn words that soothed me so deeply and beyond measure, but I know, here, now, it's a reckless thing to say.

"I was glad when social services took me to the children's ward. Got to rest."

My eyes sting, but I hold myself back. What good would my tears do for Collier?

"It's cool up here. I wish Morgan could see it…. She's gone."

We sit for a while, quiet, the other kids playing games or lifting their faces to the brightening moon as Collier tells me about their best friend Morgan. I realize all at once that this is the same girl JF was in love with, the troubled kid whose death he felt responsible for at that crazy booze- and drug-saturated party that went bad on the Canal.

Why the hell can we help strangers but not our own?

"Why do you have no hair?" Collier asks me, bringing me back to here, now.

"I had cancer."

"And that's why you've got no—"

"Life had its way with me, Collier. It does that. I'm not where I am by choice, but hey—"

"Do people ask you if you're a man or a woman?"

Collier's eyes are full on mine and I don't blink or look away.

"It's happened. Being different, it's a free ticket to mass invasion."

Collier smiles, an unguarded grin, and we share a moment of communion. I have no idea what will become of Collier or me for that matter, but for the moment, a wild wind shakes the budding branches into a gorgeous frenzy and blows through the rooftop terrace like a blessing.

PRIVATE
PRACTICE

Miri

CHART NOTES, RACHEL & NATALIE
Couple in their early forties presents for treatment in the aftermath of their teenage son's trauma. Seeks help in healing as a family. Both express sense of loss, confusion, and need a way forward.

They were holding hands. The stunner, Rachel, sat in the lotus position on my couch, her black Birks flung onto the carpet, while her partner, Natalie, slouched deep into the cushions and covered herself with one of my chenille blankets, though it hadn't turned cold yet.

"As I explained to Rachel, this is a consultation. We'll meet for an hour, and if we need to, we can schedule a second meeting. After talking to you both, I can offer a recommendation or a referral. I'm not taking on new patients right now, unfortunately, but I know many first-rate people in town who are."

They nodded in sync. Rachel had a gorgeous head of auburn hair, rippling and shining over her shoulders, and I couldn't help thinking, *In my next life, I want to be a redhead.* I was a bit tired—they were my last appointment of the day—and I took a long sip from my coconut milk latte. *Should do the trick.*

"Smells good," Natalie said with a sigh, glancing at Rachel. "I meant to get us coffees."

"So, tell me, what brings you here to see me today?" I held a Moleskine notebook in my lap, pen poised.

"You'll be taking notes on us," Rachel said—a statement, not a question. She was tall and slim in a black jersey wrap dress with a thin gold belt that accentuated her waist.

"Yes, if that's okay with you both. It helps me remember."

"Sure," Natalie said, wrapping the blanket around her shoulders like a shawl.

"It's our son, JF. That's why we're here," began Rachel, tucking her legs more tightly beneath her. "He's barely talking. To us, at least. Dawson College called the three of us in because he's cutting classes and his grades have dropped. He's in a very competitive science program and used to be a top student. We're afraid for him."

"The three of you?"

"Yeah, the two of us and his dad, Guy," explained Rachel.

"How old is JF?"

"Almost seventeen," Natalie answered.

"And when did this start, being uncommunicative, the drop in his attendance and grades?"

"Late spring, early summer," Rachel put in. "After his friend Morgan's death. Maybe you read about it in the papers?"

"I'm not sure." My belly felt like a stretched balloon that would not, could not, pop. For a minute, it was all I could think about. This bloating was happening a good deal lately, no matter what I ate or didn't eat, and I often had a pain thudding in my lower back at the same time. I made a mental note to go see my GP.

"Why don't you both tell me what happened?" I said. "Natalie?" Rachel seemed to do most of the talking and I wanted to get Natalie involved as well.

Natalie's voice was barely above a whisper, monotone; she spoke without much expression in her face, her lips barely moving to make words, her large brown eyes wide, on alert. Everyone in the room could hear my stomach acting up, gurgling and gnawing away, but Natalie and Rachel had more important things on their minds. *Focus. Be here now.* I was full of self-recriminations, which only made me more distracted, then more admonishments for not paying attention.

There'd been a party on the Lachine Canal that ran amok. Lots of drugs, alcohol, older kids crashing. A young girl died of an overdose. I remembered now reading about it in the local papers. Natalie went on to say that the girl, Morgan Rosenblum, was very important to JF.

"He was in love with her," Rachel jumped in. "His first love, really."

"So he's experienced a terrible loss," I said, knowing I was risking one of the occupational hazards of my profession, saying something obvious or dumb, something my clients already knew. Even so, this could help to put my patients' problems out there in sharp relief.

"It's way more than that," Rachel snapped, impatient with me already. "He feels *responsible* for her death."

"Makes no sense," Natalie added, shaking her head and crumpling the blanket into a ball, her olive skin darkly flushed.

"Yeah, Morgan was quite disturbed," Rachel said. "I work on the children's psych ward and I know a truly messed up kid when I see one."

"Hey there," Natalie said, nudging Rachel in the ribs. "We didn't really know her. We certainly didn't *see* her."

"Well, I heard a good deal about her from JF and—"

"Our kid's not a shining example of 'wellness' these days," Natalie said.

Rachel flipped her auburn curls over her shoulder, tilting her head slightly and looking at Natalie out of the tops of her eyes. "Why we're here, sugar."

"Okay," I said. "Tell me why JF feels responsible."

"He brought some Oxy to the party," Rachel answered. "She died of an overdose."

"I see." I took a sip of my latte and felt a bit of the bloat mercifully disperse. Lately, I was feeling more aware of my body and all of its functions, not in a good way. Surely, when I felt fine I barely noticed everything my body did for me; I just took it for granted.

Take teeth. They enabled me to bite and chew and nourish myself, but I didn't feel my teeth. Well, actually, I did. Right then, one of my molars started giving me twinges with hot and cold (the latte and the water I kept by my chair), so maybe I needed a root canal. *What's my problem today?* I bore down and paid attention. These women were here and they needed my help.

"Who knows what else was in her system?" Natalie was saying. "There were lots of drugs and alcohol at that party."

"I still don't get how JF got a hold of all that Oxy," Rachel put in.

"I was wondering the same thing," I said.

"My ex had a prescription some years back for injuries sustained in a trucking accident," Natalie explained. "Guy, JF's dad."

"You say, some years back?" I clarified.

"Guy hasn't been on that stuff for a long time," Rachel said.

"I'm not so sure," Natalie countered.

"What do you mean?" Rachel asked, sitting up straight, her torso elongated and elegant.

"He was having a lot of problems with his back this past summer. He pulled it out packing up stuff and hauling it over to the Sally Ann."

"Perhaps we could get back to JF," I coaxed, realizing that I had short-circuited Natalie's train of thought, which was most likely vital to understanding this couple's situation and dynamic, yet I pressed on. We'd get back to Natalie. "Tell me how JF was doing before this tragedy."

"Pretty good, I'd say." Rachel unraveled her lotus position and crossed one leg over the other, tucking her foot beneath the opposite ankle, forming a caduceus.

"JF excelled in science and math, played guitar and sang, went out with his pals. He had a nice group of friends. Of course, our family is a little different. There are single moms and the odd widower at his school, but we're the only family I know of with two moms."

"And a dad," added Natalie.

"When he's around."

"Is JF close to his father?"

"Do you have kids?" Rachel asked, glaring at me with large golden-brown eyes. She was confrontative, but I'd seen that before with other patients and it didn't faze me.

"This is your time."

"Well, *do* you?"

"Rach! Stop!"

I'm pretty traditional; I keep my private life private. I've chosen not to be on Facebook, Twitter, Instagram, or even LinkedIn. I know patients Google me, but they don't come up with much—maybe my APA lecture on bereavement or the one on resilience. Yet, at certain moments in therapy, disclosure makes sense and prevents a standstill. Now was one of those times.

"Yes, I am a mother. And I know how tough the teen years can be, especially sixteen through eighteen, in my experience."

Rachel backed down, a softening in her eyes and a relaxing of her posture.

"To answer your question," Natalie started, "his dad is trying, but there's a lot to make up for. Lost time, I mean. He was gone a good deal while JF was growing up, but I get that too, given the circumstances. He was kind of the odd man out."

She gave me a recap of the family's history.

"I was wondering," I asked, "did JF get invited to today's session?"

Rachel snorted; Natalie pressed her lips together.

They didn't answer. I waited.

"Since this is a consultation, maybe it's more important later on," Rachel said finally, "when we find the right person to work with him."

"He has to want to go," I emphasized. "No one can force him." Family interventions didn't always work, and with a teenager, they could backfire.

"That's the thing," Rachel added. "We're worried about what he might do—"

"To punish himself," Natalie finished Rachel's sentence.

"Has he said anything specific in that regard?"

"No!" They spoke together, an exhortation.

"We ask him constantly if he's okay," said Rachel, "even though we know the answer."

She stood up from the couch and paced around the office. "Sorry, I find it hard to sit."

"Have you specifically asked JF if he has any intention of harming himself?" I pressed, unbuttoning my blazer and laying it across the back of my chair.

When I turned around, they were looking at each other.

"I'm afraid to ask," murmured Natalie. "Don't want to put ideas in his head."

"It doesn't really work that way," I pointed out. "Raising the issue of suicide won't increase the risk. You might want to check in with him about this. You won't know what you don't know."

"We know—"

"We'll do that," Rachel interrupted Natalie. "Soon. Tonight, in fact. We'll sit him down, have a talk. Teenagers can be so impulsive."

"True," I said.

"Wait a minute...." Rachel was still standing up and looking agitated. Her behaviour was making me uncomfortable, but I wasn't going to say anything about it; it would just take us off track.

"I need to go back a bit," Rachel said. "Nat, I'm still not clear where JF got the Oxy. Guy hasn't been on medication for years."

We were back where we were before my untimely swerve. *Good.*

Natalie looked toward the door. "Could I get a glass of water? I'm parched."

I pointed her toward the washroom. She was gone a full five minutes. I sipped my latte and glanced at my notes. Rachel and I didn't speak for a while, but then she muttered, "She made a quick escape, eh?"

When Natalie came back, Rachel asked, "What's going on with Guy?"

"His back was killing him this past spring. I told you. He could barely stand or walk; sitting was the worst. I got him some medication."

"*What?*"

"From the hospital."

"Who the hell are you? Nurse Jackie!" Rachel lunged around the room, picking up a Diya statue in wood of a warrior queen made by the Berbers, which I'd brought back from a trip to Marrakesh. I bit my lip, but kept quiet. She took a dismissive look at the statue and then placed it back hastily, not exactly in the same position.

"I got a limited supply—for *Guy*. He got off painkillers after he recovered from his accident. I knew he wouldn't abuse them this time. I trust him."

Rachel, still standing, pressed the fingertips of her right hand against her forehead, as if she had a pain there, her elbow akimbo, and then yanked upward, and the gorgeous red hair ripped off her skull and hung from a clawed fist, waves catching the overhead light in glints of auburn and gold.

I gasped. I didn't mean to; it just came out.

She had a downy fuzz of indeterminate colour on her nearly bald head.

"I've been sick," she said. "I've had breast cancer—twice, in fact. I'm done my treatment and I'm back at work, but this is too much. I've been trying to get better while JF is going off the rails, and now I find out that *you*," she was yelling now, "stole opioids from the hospital to give to *Guy*? What the hell were you thinking, Nat? *Not!*" Her amber eyes expanded. "Are you fucking him?"

Natalie had tears in her eyes. "Rachel, please."

Rachel was a rather threatening figure, standing tall and erect in the centre of my consulting room holding that red wig aloft like a deranged Shakespearean queen.

"Ms. Neuman."

"Don't Ms. Neuman—"

"Rachel, I see you're very angry, that you've been through the ringer. But if we're to continue here today, you need to lower your voice and calm down. I insist on that."

She dropped the red wig onto a side table. "Fuck it! I swore I wouldn't *ever* wear one of these." She scratched hard at her downy scalp with uncontained fury. "They're hot! And itchy. I didn't want the focus to be on *me* today."

Natalie laughed low in her throat. "Well, you've done a great job of *not* making the focus on *you*, Rach!"

"I didn't want to have to talk about me having been sick, a cancer quote, unquote survivor," Rachel went on. "It always sucks all the air out of the room. Cancer. And please, don't call it a journey or a battle—it's my fucking cells gone rogue! And hell," she pointed at the splayed red wig, "this is just like my original hair BC."

"Before cancer," Natalie said, reaching for Rachel's hand and coaxing her back onto the couch. Once Rachel had settled down, Natalie put her arm around her partner and Rachel leaned against Natalie's strong, wide shoulder.

I thought that BC could also mean before children. And said something to that effect.

"That too," Rachel said. "I got my first bout of breast cancer shortly after JF's birth. Great timing, right?"

"I'm so sorry."

"I don't know if I really know you," Rachel whispered to Natalie, ignoring me.

"Of course you do."

"Well, what's going on with you and Guy?"

"Nothing, *that* way. He's a great friend and the father of our son. Hello! How could you even think that? But he was in such pain." She adjusted her position on the couch, sidling away from Rachel. "I feel responsible for this girl's death too."

Rachel shook her head and everyone was quiet for a while.

"Are we going to tell JF about this?" Rachel asked. "Do you think it would help? Take the onus off him?"

They both turned to me, awaiting my response. Despite everything they were going through, these women were clearly cherished by each other, probably by their son as well, and even by the father of their child.

"There's a lot going on here," I said finally, something I try never to say because it's a given with each and every client that walks through my door. I wasn't at my best during this appointment, clearly having an off day.

"I understand your concern about JF, but there are lots of issues to work out in the family as well." Now I was making some sense.

Rachel nodded. "We thought it would all be just perfect."

I wasn't sure what she was referring to, but Natalie explained without my having to ask.

"Yeah," she said. "The two of us together. And JF."

"And then life happened," I said. "I feel your closeness and connection," I went on. "I can tell that you've been through a lot all at once, which can make anyone feel overwhelmed. And angry. But it's hard to know where to aim that rage. Your bond is going to be a positive force in helping JF and healing your family."

Natalie spread the blanket over both her and Rachel's knees. "She just gets cold," Natalie said. "After all the cancer treatment."

"And hot," Rachel put in.

"You *are* hot," Natalie said, and they nodded, laughing, in a moment of respite.

I smiled wanly, uncomfortable, and fiddled with my necklace, a gift from my late partner Levin. My mind wandered for a moment, wondering if I would ever have another relationship—or if I would ever have sex again! I missed Levin; I missed my two young adult kids, Max and Bella, who were both in New York starting out their careers. I struggled to block out the tiny barbed sting of envy I felt for these women and the love they shared and then I strained to overcome my shame about having those feelings. A voice inside my head murmured, *You're human. Doctors are people. Even shrinks.* I chuckled without meaning to.

They both looked up at me as if I'd gone mad. I glanced at the clock. We still had a little time. I needed to think. *Should I try to get this whole family in here for another session?* No, that wasn't realistic and it might just conflagrate an already combustible situation. Surely, the dad felt some responsibility for this girl's death too. Shared guilt did not necessarily mitigate its weight for individuals who held themselves responsible. Guilt was complex.

And not always a bad thing. I was unnerved by Natalie's confession about stealing opioids from the hospital. But by now, after several decades in practice, I'd seen and heard it all. I didn't think she would do it again. *What am I, law enforcement?*

"We're almost out of time for today," I said, a bit too curtly, my voice loud in the quiet. "Is there anything else you'd like me to know?"

"Well, just if you think Nat should tell JF that she was the one who supplied the Oxy."

"I can't weigh in on that today," I said. "Though it seems like it would be an easy fix, I don't think it would help JF as much as you might hope."

"What will?" Rachel asked. "Help him, I mean."

"Time. I know it's a cliché, but it has the force of truth behind it. And therapy."

"Right," Natalie said.

"Your whole family might benefit from talking to someone," I said. "And I have a person in mind for you. His name is Nico Tesoro."

"Is he a shrink?" Natalie asked.

"No. He's a social worker, MSW, a brilliant one. Nico is amazing with teens. He's a bit unorthodox at times, but he has a knack for finding what works in even the most difficult and painful circumstances."

"Unorthodox how?" Natalie asked.

Like she should be asking.

"Nothing transgressive or damaging, of course," I said. "If a kid is restless, Nico might do their session outdoors. Sometimes, he'll take a client to a café. He would be able to see JF individually but also meet with your family. In addition, he runs groups for teens." I stood, got out my pad, and wrote out the referral, handing it to Rachel.

"Yeah," she said, "I think I've heard of him."

"I'll let Nico know you'll be getting in touch. If you come up with any questions, feel free to give me a call," I said, still standing. "Thanks for coming in this afternoon."

Rachel stood, and then Natalie got up slowly, as if reluctant to leave. I crouched to pick up the wig of shining auburn curls from the end table; it wasn't so beautiful now that it was separated from a human head. I held it out toward Rachel.

"Keep it," she said with a warm and winning smile, her amber eyes shining. She was beautiful with or without hair. "A souvenir to remember us by."

They were out the door and down the stairs before I could protest. I went into my bathroom and fitted the wig over my own hair, looking at myself in the mirror. *Nope, not a good look.* Red hair clashed with my olive colouring and made me look clownish. Pulling it off, I hung it on the coat rack and then finger-combed my dark brown hair and applied a bit of burgundy lipstick. *Sometimes nature just got it right.* I headed out into the brilliant autumn afternoon.

BROTHER'S
KEEPER

Adán

Their old telepathy, now it was Adán's curse. He heard the jarring
ring shudder through dreams before the phone actually sounded.
Signs of his older brother's sickness seeped through his pores, tensing
his shoulders. Inside where he slept with his *novia,* Julieta, Adán
rubbed sleep-crusted eyes, an ache starting in his head. It was hot,
dark, damp. Rain dripped and poured out of the heavy Tortuguero
air. Even the howler monkeys were not yet awake.

Julieta rolled over, flopping onto her stomach and Adán felt the
bedsprings vibrate under her considerable weight. Nineteen years
together, since they were thirteen, more brother and sister than lovers.
Adán's skin felt cold, clammy, and damp as he picked up the phone.

"*Ayúdame,*" whined Joaquin, "*ayúdame.*"

Adán longed for their *old* telepathy, reading his brother's thoughts,
saying the same words in sync, planning schemes—Joaquín daring
and wild, Adán sidekick and protector.

"La Fundación is crumbling down around me," sniffled Joaquín. "I
am all alone, in stagnation, do you know what this means?"

Adán sighed.

"*Hermano,* another director down the toilet. You must come.
Now. You promised me!"

Adán knew there would be whole days to get through now,
absorbing the force of Joaquín's melodramatic emotions. He hung
up—what good was talk?—and dressed quickly.

Julieta would help Mami at the Super Morpho Pulpería, their general store. Adán could be at La Fundación de la Tierra Primera by afternoon to bail his brother out and stay as long as it took to set things right. The invisible thread that bound them was pulled taut, a noose.

Adán rattled up the dirt road to La Fundación in his beat-up, black pickup. It was early January and the Costa Rican rainy season had just ended with an explosive abundance of fruits and flowers, the natural embodiment of deafening rain and blinding light. Everything around Adán glistened—buttery blooms, the brilliant scarlet and green of heliconia, pink and purple bougainvillea.

As he walked about the moist hills, he was enveloped by the scents of wild plants, flowers, and ripe mangoes, which released their aromatic juices as they rotted in the path along with papayas and plantains. Seeing the rotting fruit, his sense of dread heightened.

In the past year, three directors had come and gone at La Fundación, this vast farm-estate Joaquín's late lover, Dr. Antony Fortesque, had founded as a centre for conservationists, sponsoring them in projects to protect Costa Rica's natural resources. The centre had thrived during Dr. Fortesque's life, as had Joaquín, its only artist, his wood sculptures adorning the grounds and *la casa grande,* handsome Joaquín, the centre's jewel. Adán knew his older brother had done his best work under the warm bright beam of Antony's belief in him... but now that light had gone out.

Adán started as a coconut fell on the roof of one of the cottages with a loud crack. The land had been neglected for some time, wild and overgrown. He breathed in deeply, girding himself up, before facing his brother.

The door was open to *la casa grande* where Joaquín had lived with Antony Fortesque. He had come so far from their house of greyish, weather-beaten boards on stilts in Tortuguero village. Adán crept inside like a thief. A chocolate lab puppy tore up to him, wagging his tail. He picked the dog up in his arms and carried him as he walked around the place. Dishes were piled in the sink, ants caught in smears of jam on the counter. The sharp, fusty smell of urine mixed with stale cat litter assailed him.

Adán found his brother Joaquín in a heavy sleep upstairs, the airy bedroom littered with dirty clothes, soiled linen, old plates of food, and empty liquor bottles. The only well-kept place was the dresser top, now a makeshift altar: dried flowers wreathed about photographs of Joaquín and a handsome, silver-haired man with translucent eyes and chiselled cheekbones, carefully arranged around a group of talismans and surrounded by white candles.

Adán's throat went dry as he shook Joaquín's shoulder. He grabbed his brother's phone and put on salsa, top volume.

"*Ayúdame*," whined Joaquín again, "help me, *hermano*."

"You are thirty-five years old! You should know better."

Joaquín groaned, cursed, while Adán cleaned up the house in a whirlwind; disgusted, he dragged Joaquín from his bed and stood him up in the shower.

In the world they'd grown up in, being a *puto* was worse than being a *borracho*, but both, one couldn't get much lower. Adán was puzzled by and ashamed of his brother's inclinations, man enough to be ashamed of being ashamed.

As Joaquín slipped into a silk kimono, Adán put on a pot of coffee. They sat across from each other on the veranda, looking out over the valley. The little chocolate lab puppy came over to Adán, nuzzling his leg, and Adán picked him up in his arms as the pup licked his earlobe.

"Do you have a name?"

"Bonbón," said Joaquín, his voice clotted with sleep and hangover.

"Why don't you take care of him?"

Joaquín shrugged.

"Oh, I forgot, you can't take care of yourself." Adán felt the poison rush through Joaquin's blood as if through his own veins; anger was driving him crazy.

Joaquín had always been the handsome one—lanky, with mink-black hair, flashing black eyes, and smooth olive skin, but his dissolute life had taken its toll. Adán could see he was too thin, but flabby from lack of activity. His skin had a yellowish tinge and his eyes were dull. At thirty-two, Adán was nearly bald and missing a front tooth from a childhood fall. He was shorter and thicker than Joaquín with a workmanlike build, which easily put on both weight and muscle. His face was weathered from work and sun and many thought him closer to forty. He didn't pay much attention to his looks, but he liked his eyes, which were blueish grey and stood out against his tanned skin.

"It is descending," Joaquín mumbled.

"What?" Adán sipped his coffee. "The plague?"

"Worse, the people." Joaquín smiled wanly. "You know, *hermano*, the conservationists with their Projects and Ideas, their Important Opinions, their *grandes expectativas*. I cannot face them."

"Face yourself."

"Don't try to be clever, it's not in your character. Oh, what do they *want* from me?"

That snivelling again, worse than nails scratching a blackboard.

"I'm sure they are not all that interested in *you*, *hermano*. They will be thrilled to be in our beautiful *país*, an opportunity to do their work. Read the brochure you sent to me so many years ago." Adán refilled their cups with coffee. "So what are the projects this year?"

Joaquín sighed melodramatically. "Do you think I care?"

"You should."

"So many shoulds, always."

"We must clean up this place. You should look for a new manager or take charge of things."

That signature groan again.

"Once La Fundación is back—standing—it will be easier to find a new manager."

Adán jumped up and went inside the house, looking in cabinets, drawers, and under beds until he found all of his brother's caches, dumped the bottles, and took them outside. "Cold turkey is the best; it is the only way."

Joaquín dropped his head on the kitchen table, cradling it in his arms.

"If you don't care, go back to San José. Be a waiter… or a whore!"

"I could never sell this place. Every night I speak to Antony *en mis sueños. La vida es sueño, hermano, ¿recuerdas?*"

"So you think life is a dream? I don't want to hear *sus detalles cochinos.*"

"I am not dirty! *Palabras grandes, hermano y crueles.* Where did you learn such harsh words?"

Adán flashed Joaquín a toxic look.

"I love Antony still, so hard to go on alone." Joaquín lifted his face and looked at Adán, his expression worn, tragic.

Adán wiped wet from his brother's face.

"I am here now. It will be different."

Darkness closed in by six, a blackout, sudden as a swoon. Unable to sleep, Adán listened to the wind, alive, an animate presence; it shushed through the brush and filled the lungs of the palms, wildly shaking leaves, flowers, fruit. Bamboo clacked like castanets, then the hollow branches squealed in a sound almost human. The wind rose in waves, building to crescendo, a wild storming, without rain.

At dawn, Adán heard church bells, the roosters, and dogs. He worked hard—he was used to it—and within a few weeks the grounds, trees, and cottages were in good shape. He found a village woman to do the housework and prepare meals; Joaquín promised to lead the excursions.

Five of the conservationists arrived the first and second of February, looking as if they had stepped from a black-and-white world into one of living colour. Joaquín, pale and shaky himself, turned them over like hotcakes to Adán. One more was expected, a young woman from somewhere up north in Canada. Adán checked the list: Katie Mathews. He asked Joaquín about her and his brother shrugged.

At the end of the first week, on his way back from the village, Adán spotted a young woman dragging a large duffel bag up the steep, winding road that led back to the grounds of La Fundación. He pulled over in his pickup.

"Can I give you some help?"

Her eyes rested on Adán's for a moment.

"I'm looking for La Fundación de la Tierra Primera," she said, her voice clear, bell-like. "I had a taxi; we drove around for an hour. The man... he was weird, and I was getting freaked out. So I bailed." Adán let out a laugh of pleasure he scarcely understood and soon regretted. "Most know the place."

She scowled, then dumped the duffel bag, dust billowing at her feet.

"You are Katie?" Adán asked, getting out of his pickup.

She stepped back a pace, caution in her clear green eyes.

"Katie Mathews?" He put out his hand, palm open. "I am the groundskeeper at La Fundación, Adán Herrera. My brother, Joaquín, is director now."

"Oh," she sighed deeply, her slender body bending forward, as she shook out sore wrists and hands. Katie was tall and graceful, no more than eighteen, with thick masses of honey-coloured hair bound in two pigtails and rippling over her shoulders.

"Let me help you," Adán said, lifting the case in one motion and placing it into the bed of his pickup. Katie stretched back in her seat, drawing a crumpled sheet of paper from her pocket, crackling it open.

"So, you don't use street names or numbers?"

Adán laughed. "Not even in San José."

"Just relative terms?"

"Landmarks also. Your cab driver, he should already be used to this. *La cuarta entrada de los yoses, por ejemplo.* The fourth entrance in the neighbourhood of the Yos tree. Street addresses, they will not help you here."

"Ahhh," she said, "I'll keep that in mind."

"Where are you from?" he asked.

"Montreal, though my dad lives in Newfoundland. I'm there more now, since my mom died."

"I'm so sorry."

Katie was quiet for a long while.

"And what is your kind of study?" Adán felt awkward, struggling with English. Often, he fished for words, the *right* word in the right moment, and when he found it, he rejoiced.

"I'll be working at the refuge for nesting sea turtles at La Playa Barra de Matina and the green turtle research station started by Archie Carr. You know it?"

"Tortuguero, this is my home village."

"Cool."

"Have you been to my country before?"

"My dad took me when I was ten; I got to watch the sea turtles. Dad promised me our next visit I could bring my friend JF." She let out a deep sigh of pleasure. "I'd never seen anything like those sea turtles."

Adán talked more, the radio on, but when he glanced over at Katie, she was asleep. Soon they arrived at La Fundación and he shook her gently awake.

Adán looked after the ample grounds while the conservationists immersed themselves in their projects. Soon Joaquín was back to his binges.

It was Adán who drove the residents to the village for their groceries so they would not have to climb the steep hill laden with packages and he also planned the excursions, hiring two assistants to cover the farm work.

The group needed to make a trip to Tortuguero, Adán's home village; a number would do field work there. Adán told Joaquín he would be leading a longer excursion and he set off for the northern Caribbean coast with Benjamin, who was working to preserve the rain forest; Luz, who planned to study the behaviour of the howler monkeys; and Katie, with her project on the nesting sea turtles.

They climbed northward on the Guápiles Highway, cutting through the Parque Nacional Braulio Carrillo. The highway was one of the most dangerous in the country, its steep hills shrouded in mist and fog; rock and mud slides common. The trip would take a good part of the day, at least four hours in the jeep, much of it climbing winding back roads. Heading to his home village, Adán felt sadness and yearning beneath every breath.

As the ferry idled nearing the dock at their lodge, The Pachira, he asked Katie, "When will your work begin?"

"Next week, preliminary research, anyway. I'll stay on for the leatherbacks, the green turtles, and the hawksbill."

"So you will remain—"

"At least through September."

"So this is your time," Adán said, and she smiled, full-lipped, her eyes on his.

A guide showed them to their rooms. Adán liked the remote feeling in their part of the lodge, which was called Evergreen, each cabin like a private treehouse tucked into the rain forest equipped with a porch and back veranda, hammocks, and rocking chairs for lounging.

He sat on the bed, hands folded in his lap. Outside the large-screened window, he could see the jungle—spider monkeys playing in the trees, sunlight dropping through the branches and lush, wet greens. Being alone in this room was new, strange. Though Adán had been on Sunday picnics with Joaquín and Mami, a day for fishing or swimming, he had never taken a trip for pure pleasure, a vacation. He felt an unfamiliar buoyancy, a shard of fear. *He should stop in on Mami, but then he would see Julieta; they would ask about Joaquín.*

He was home and not home.

Adán awoke early to the caterwauling roar of the howler monkeys. He and Katie set out on the olive-brown canals in a small skiff, dressed in ponchos and rubber boots, their heads covered in clear plastic hoods. The day was terribly hot with intermittent, drenching showers.

"I wanted to come back each year," she said, "but there was never the money or the time."

"I love the sea turtles," said Adán. "As boys, Joaquín and I would go late into the night to watch *la arribada*. I remember one; she must have been over one hundred pounds. Bigger than the both of us together! She crawled out of the sea at two o'clock in the morning onto the black sands. She had swum thousands of miles, of this I am sure."

"I remember," Katie went on, "the mother using her flippers to dig a huge pit—that pit could hold a dozen people! She crouched, heaving, with constant sighs, her eyes shedding large tears. I was just ten years old. I cried too."

"Very few survive."

"But some *must*."

Adán smiled.

"The mother covered her nest with a blanket of sand," Katie went on, "and lumbered back to the water. Two months later, we saw her hatchlings race to sea. It's amazing to think, when I'm, I don't know, like, forty, I'll see some of the same hatchlings I saw when I was ten, nesting, laying their own eggs on that beach."

Adán nodded, pointing out a spectacled caiman family and a Jesus Christ lizard, who walked upright on the water. Katie's eyes brightened, and he felt himself come alive, seeing his old familiar world through her eyes.

"I've been able to study," she was saying. "Then I got this fellowship; it's such a gift. I feel like I'm just beginning."

Adán smiled at her.

"I told my friend JF about it hoping he'd apply too. JF's really smart. But he's not doing so good. Me neither some days. I miss my mom. I don't know what to do with all the love I have for her, where to put it. Sometimes, I forget she's gone. I think I'll tell her something. Then I remember."

"Can I ask you when she passed?"

"She didn't pass. She was hit by a car. It's been two years already. Maybe she's watching me. It's comforting to think that."

"Yes, yes, I believe the dead are real, that they inhabit the living." Katie smiled at him.

"You have your whole life out before you," Adán said, newly mesmerized by the steamy mystique of the canals, aware only of the small skiff's chugging engine, the flash of wings as birds stalked bugs, and the sudden splashes in the turgid waters. At sunset, they docked and strolled along the Caribbean coast of his boyhood, with its grey waves, log-strewn shores, and mud-moist sand. It was here that she would do her field work with the nesting turtles.

There was barely time to change before dinner. Adán showered quickly and knocked on Katie's door. At dinner he spoke of their day, of his childhood, and a Spanish group invited everyone after supper to "*Tomar algo*" at the bar.

Sitting beside Katie near the aquamarine water of the pool, Adán sipped rum and listened to salsa. The night had cooled and he was enjoying the breeze on his face and bare arms. He watched it lift Katie's honey-coloured hair, now streaked with gold, wafting it around her face. She had gotten a bit of a sunburn, her cheeks pink, mosquito bites on the backs of her hands.

Soon the band started a limbo contest. Two young Ticos held the bamboo branch as the music started up. Katie rose from her chair and grabbed Adán's hand, pulling him up.

"No, I cannot do this." He felt his skin prickle with heat. "I am no good for this."

She pulled harder, and he was surprised by her strength, as he rose to his feet, laughing.

"I am too old," he protested to Katie. Adán thought of his lower back—which throbbed with pain after a week's work at La Fundación, not daring to imagine what limbo would do to it—his knees which were giving him trouble, and his middle starting to sag slightly over his belt.

Katie looked directly into his face and kept her eyes on him. He looked away, and she touched his upper arm under his t-shirt, spreading a sudden warmth through him.

"Let's do this," she said under her breath, her voice a husky whisper, tugging Adán toward the line of people who were ready to limbo, her green eyes glowing in the delicate fairy lights by the pool.

The limbo music filled his ears, familiar and catchy, as they circled, taking turns, going under the bamboo branch. There were nine of them—five men, four women. The men were clowning around. One was bald and fat, sticking his wide behind out and wiggling it as he made his way toward the pole, and another was dressed in a woman's pink bikini, with beefy hair-covered arms and legs. There was an American teenager in baggy Hawaiian-print trunks holding a can of beer, whose buddies were jeering at him from the bar, and finally, a well-mannered newlywed, dressed in a crisp white shirt and snug black jeans, who kept a close eye on his young wife.

Adán felt giddy and reckless, a combination of sensations he hadn't experienced since he and Joaquín slipped a green spiny lizard down Señora Molina's white blouse in grade three. He watched the women, particularly Katie. She was graceful, surprisingly good, given her height and the slenderness of her limbs. They circled round after round. The bald, fat man knocked the pole over on purpose with his bottom, and then Adán was out. He got himself another drink and watched. Soon the young married man was eliminated and it was only the women and this loud young American left. Adán couldn't take his eyes off Katie, the way her bare arms and legs glowed and her breasts rose as she arched her back, her hair cascading to the floor. He drank, smoked cigarette after cigarette. After a while, it was just Katie and the young American. The boy was quite drunk and weaved his way unsteadily, knocking over the pole. Katie won and jumped up and down like a little girl. The bandleader took her by the wrist and thrust her slender white arm into the air. She won a small trophy and a couple of free drinks.

Adán went to her, smiling. Sweat glistened on her face and between her breasts. She looked so happy. They took their drinks to the deserted pool and settled on the edge of a chaise longue, their drinks on the ground beside them.

"How did you get so good?"

She shrugged. "I just throw myself back and hope for the best."

"So are you ready to get to work?"

"You've brought this place to life, helped me understand it."

Adán looked down. Before he had come to La Fundación, he felt he'd lost his direction, but in showing her his world, he'd found a new purpose. He didn't know how to express any of this in English.

"Will you stay at La Fundación?" she asked. "With your brother?"

"I don't know. Tortuguero is home, yet.... I'm not sure what is here for me—the Pulpería, Mami, but—"

"Many nights, I'm homesick, but for what I can't say." She took a deep breath, a sip of her rum, then patted his knee. He felt the warmth still, even after she withdrew her hand.

They were both quiet for a while. When Adán looked back at the bar, the band had packed up and many of the tourists had returned to the lodges. Just a few lone drinkers remained at the bar, and the pool, tremulous and shimmering, was empty.

"When I think of home," Katie said, her voice soft and melancholy, "I feel this loneliness seep into my blood. I miss home, my mom, but don't know where home is anymore."

He had felt much the same, but leaving and then coming back with her had changed his perspective. "This is a special place. *Rico.*"

Suddenly, without warning, she peeled off her damp shorts and t-shirt, then dove into the pool, leaving a diamond-bright geyser behind her. She swam the length of the pool without coming up for air. Adán watched but didn't join her. When Katie surfaced, she looked at him and he said, "The whole pool, it is for you."

She went underwater again and he stood by as she swam. When Adán saw her dunk her head backward into the pool and wring out her hair, he moved swiftly to the cabana and took several towels for her. As Katie emerged, he felt a sudden shyness and turned away, and she took the towels gratefully from the foot of the chaise where he'd left them.

When Adán looked up, she had wrapped one in her hair, turban like, and a second around her body under her arms. He could see the half-moons of her breasts over the towel, her skin's wet gleam.

Though the day had been terribly hot, there was a breeze now through the jungle, rippling the water. The wind felt good on Adán's face, neck, and arms, but Katie's lips were blue.

"Come," he said, his voice low, his arm in a shepherding sweep around her. "You will get sick from this chill."

Adán guided Katie through the criss-cross of pathways and the dark glinting trees and heliconia back to Evergreen. The canal gave off a steamy wet smell, heavy and brackish. They stood in the amber light of the veranda, the jungle all around with its night sounds and smells.

Adán felt his mouth go dry. He leaned down and took Katie's damp, pale face in his hands, cradling it, kissing her cheeks, then her lips. She held his wrists, kissing back, but restraining his touch. The towel in her hair unravelled, tumbling into his arms. He let go of her and flung it to the floor. The thirst he felt was terrible, the sweetness of rum mixing with the ashy aftertaste of cigarettes. Katie was shivering, a scared look on her face.

"Okay," he said softly, "enough." In truth, he was scared too.

He gathered her into him, then gently kissed the top of her head. Katie ducked quickly into her room and Adán waited for the sliding bolt of her lock. Tomorrow, he would return to La Fundación, while Katie and the others stayed on for their field work. He felt a sudden chill, a shadow moving over him.

Adán got back to La Fundación late at night and floated to his cottage. Though his limbs were heavy and sore and his back ached, he felt happy, a healthy tiredness. He looked forward to a long hot shower, to clean cool sheets. His mind wandered back over Tortuguero, daydreaming about Katie. As he stepped onto the porch, Joaquín lunged at him from the shadows. Adán jumped, catching his brother before he fell. Joaquín's breath was sweetly stale—old wine, beer, and dried sweat.

"¿Qué pasa?"

"Where have you been?" Joaquín reeled toward Adán, grabbing him by the collar of his shirt, wobbling as he struggled to hold him.

Adán wrenched free and Joaquín fell backward against the wooden door. He pushed himself back up, bracing himself against the porch railing.

"You know where I have been. Doing *your* job, leading the excursions."

"Excursions? That is a nice word for it. *Eres un puto porque dejaste tu trabajo por una mujer.*"

A guttural sound came from Adán's throat, half laugh, half growl. "Don't make me laugh! Look at you. Every day of your life, you do not do your work. You are lazy, wasting your time, not for a woman, *verdad,* but for every white *machillo* you are digging out from under a rock. You disgust me. You are handsome and smart, *hermano,* more handsome and smart than me. You could be anything you choose, and what do you choose? Waste."

Adán grabbed his slender, drunken brother by the shoulders and shook him hard. "Wake up! Wake up before it is too late for you. *Maricón. ¡Maricón!*"

Joaquín's wail spiralled upward. He sprang free, his high hard laugh indistinguishable from a scream.

"We are the same!" he cried suddenly. "We are the same!"

Joaquín's words burrowed under Adán's skin.

"What are you talking about?"

"You know what I am saying, *hermano.* You are a *puta.* Sucking up to these conservationists, day and night, becoming their servant. Pretending to be one of them at the same time. I mean, look at you! You left your *novia,* our home. You are a whore as much as me. Pretending to be something you are not. No nice brown Tica for you, only a *blanca,* a nice white *Americana con pelo rubio.*"

"She is Canadian. And her hair is light brown."

"Canadian, American, what's the difference?"

Adán felt his rage come up, hot and sudden, his skin prickling with heat. His hands spanned his brother's head, were around his throat, squeezing. Adán felt the pulsing life in Joaquín's neck, the fibrous, sinewy tendons, tough as rope, as he imagined a bare-throated tiger heron, its neck twisted, and for a moment, his grip loosened.

Joaquín choked, bending, and picked up the machete, which rested against the corner of the porch, where Adán had left it after a day's work on the farm. When Joaquín stood, the curved blade of the machete glimmered dully in the yellow porchlight. As boys, Adán and Joaquín had wandered the sweltering maze of canals, swamps, beaches, and forests of Tortuguero wielding that machete. They had stalked jaguars and cougars, roamed the wet, mud-brown sand strewn with sargassum seaweed, driftwood, and coconuts, which they collected and sold to tourists. Adán bored holes through the shell, while Joaquín handed each person a straw. If the tourists liked coconut meat, the brothers fought over the machete; one or the other hacked the coconut open and into pieces for the group. Then there was always the photograph, the two brothers holding the machete, along with a middle-aged man, paunchy and sunburned, arms around one another. And a few coins thrown at them.

"Put that down, *loco*."

With a trembling hand, Joaquín lifted the long, curved blade and held it against Adán's throat. Adán kept his eyes on his brother, feeling the wet gleam of the knife; a muscle in his neck twitched.

"I will cut your white face," Joaquín threatened, "*gabacho.*"

"My face is not white."

Adán felt the heat of his brother's breath on him; his own heart pounded in his chest. Or was that Joaquín's?

"Do you remember our explorations, *hermano?*" Adán whispered. "Everything we saw and found together. How we played. We have come so far, too far from home."

Adán saw Joaquín's hand trembling hard, and the machete shook and fell, grazing Adán's thigh. He cried out, cursing.

Adán propped Joaquín against the front door, then pulled his t-shirt over his head and wrapped it tightly around his own leg to staunch the bleeding.

"Lean on me," Adán said, putting an arm around Joaquín. Joaquín crumpled against Adán, and in one motion, Adán lifted Joaquín in his arms and carried him into the cottage, limping on his wounded leg. As he stumbled into the warm, neat bedroom, his brother's breath against his cheek, Joaquín's eyes closing, Adán thought about what would come. The rest of the conservationists would pack up and leave soon for their field work. Joaquín would sleep through his days with his wine, beer, and lovers until La Fundación fell apart. A wealthy expat would purchase the property and retire there or use the place to implement some dream of his or her own. Joaquín would fall, tumble and fall, until he could fall no further. Then he would claw his way back up or.... Adán could not think about the alternative. Adán would leave too. He would go back home to Tortuguero, but he would have a different life there. He would speak to Julieta, tell her the truth. She deserved that; it would be easier now that he'd made the break. Adán would work on his English, get his training to be a tour guide. Mami would be so proud.

As he lay his brother, who was nearly weightless, onto the bed, rain gushed from the sky, enveloping Adán in its roar, not unlike the sea. A glow warmed his insides as he saw himself in the deepest part of the night on a long stretch of black sand, watching a huge leatherback rise from the sea. He will explain to the awed group that she has swum thousands of miles to her *own* birthplace, to lay her eggs. If at this moment she hears unfamiliar noises, sees light or movement, she will be frightened back to the water and deposit her eggs into the open seas where they will be nothing but game. Adán will watch, listen, as the sea turtle crouches in her nest. He'll hear her heaves and grunts, watch the zigzag stream of tears squeezed from her squinting eyes. When she finishes, she'll swing her flippers, delicately, rhythmically in a backward motion, dusting her eggs with a blanket of sand. Then she will lumber back to the waves, which will welcome her, whisking her out to sea.

HOW DID THIS
BECOME *My*
LIFE?

JF

MY FUNERAL SONGS

"1-800-273-8255"—Logic
"Everybody Hurts"—R.E.M.
"Jump Around"—House of Pain

It felt good not to feel. JF adjusted his position on the snowbank, scribbling into the notebook that his therapist Nico Tesoro had given him at their first session. It was hardbacked with lines; it had heft. The numbness crept from his ass and the backs of his thighs down through his calves and ankles all the way to his toes, and then back up, settling deep in his chest. His heart hurt, fingers cramped from writing in the cold.

He wished they'd both be numb. How could the worst be yet to come?

Since Morgan's death seven months ago, his anxiety had become physical: less space for air in his lungs; his breath caught, half-full, half-empty. He couldn't eat or sleep for more than a couple of hours, awakening in the dark at three or four a.m. covered with a slick of sweat, his heart pounding, mind spinning.

His loss had turned to dread. Each day seemed endless with no forward momentum, no belief that he would ever feel any different.

JF wondered if it would be better if he were dead. Suicide presented itself as a potential solution.

Nico had broached this topic with him and checked in often, unlike his moms who talked around it, mute with fear.

JF had thought about simply *not* being, the bliss and peace of that state, free of pain, but a real mensch had to get down to specifics. How would he do it? Pills were the easiest for sure, the most comfortable, and he would be in solidarity with Morgan.

He'd scoped out the medicine cabinet at home and ransacked his moms' separate night tables on either side of their bed while they were at work, carefully replacing everything as it was, or how he remembered it being organized.

All of the sleeping pills and benzos had been cleared away. On a visit to his dad, he discovered the same deal. No Oxy, no benzos, no sleeping pills—not even a bottle of Percocet.

Hanging was the macho way to go. Usually this was done in basements or attics, right? Well, they didn't have either one in his apartment. Also, a side effect was shitting and pissing yourself. Did he really want his moms to find him like that? And it hardly seemed a painless or surefire way to go. What if you half-strangled yourself? Then what?

When he was about ten years old, the father across the street had killed himself by asphyxiation. Lester Berman shut himself inside his car in the garage and ran a pipe from the exhaust directly into the vehicle. Carbon dioxide is odourless and colourless and tasteless and will cause reasonably swift unconsciousness. On discovery, the body will look peaceful.

Of course, JF didn't figure out these details about his neighbour until later on. His moms told him that Lester had incurable cancer. They weren't super close with Lester or his family, but it was still a shocker when JF found out the truth from the word on the street, eventually confirmed by Lester's widow, Gail. Lester left behind not only his wife and his parents, but two cute young kids—a girl of five, and a boy, seven—as well as a gorgeous Bernese mountain dog.

Before he died, JF had often spotted Lester shut inside his garage, solo, working on mysterious projects, ordering food in late at night, usually from some chicken joint. He was busy in the yard as well, sprinkling grass seed and planting lilac bushes, daffodils, and tulips. He was always doing something, which wasn't the way JF pictured a suicidal person. Lester's death remained a conundrum. Maybe he was depressed and empty, like JF felt now, and coped with it by keeping super occupied. Until he didn't.

During the holiday season, a few months after Lester's death, JF and his mom Natalie stopped by the house with a box of cookies they'd baked. The two kids and their Berner were out in the yard building a snowman. Gail invited JF and his mom in for tea and just started talking; clearly she needed to talk—badly.

"Cancer?" she said. "How did that rumour get started?"

JF's mom Natalie glanced at him with fear and shook her head hard, but Gail barrelled ahead like a runaway train.

"Lester killed himself. He was depressed his whole life. Born sad."

The asphyxiation route wouldn't work for JF. No one in the family owned a car, for starters.

Readjusting his position on the snowbank, sitting cross-legged now, JF remembered how he used to feel more a part of things, his family, classmates, the whole fucking human race. He'd had friends. There were long talks over recess with Katie Mathews about the migrating sea turtles, which she knew endless fun facts about—such as their ability to travel as far as eight thousand miles and live to nearly a hundred—and he'd often jammed with Tony's band in the evenings and learned a three-finger technique from him on electric guitar, going out with the group for poutine and Cokes afterward, or beers if they weren't carded. But his obsession with Morgan had expanded, little by little, taking up so much space in his mind, heart, and being that there was little room for anything or anyone else. He found himself isolated and alone. A pinball aimlessly shooting and bouncing off walls, going nowhere.

Yet his obsession with Morgan was probably the most interesting thing about him.

JF felt an invisible pull, welcoming surrender to a force that felt outside of himself. Sliding down the snowbank, he walked, creaky and frozen at first, then more agile, until he was standing in front of Morgan's house beside the pretty pocket park blanketed in snow. She'd lived in this sprawling white Victorian with its pale pink trim, its turrets and tower room, a house like a fairy-tale castle or a fussy wedding cake. He needed to be inside the house where Morgan had lived, inside the room where she'd slept.

There were no cars in the driveway and JF rang the bell. A petite woman answered the door and he started talking before he could think of what to say.

"I'm a student of Professor Rosenblum's, left my music here, the other day."

Just as he got words out, a plumbing truck pulled into the driveway and a big man hoisted himself out, heralding his arrival with a clanging belt of tools.

"¡Por Dios!" the woman called out. "The problem is upstairs."

The plumber walked in and JF trailed close behind. He saw water sluicing down through the high living room ceiling, dripping from the pear-shaped crystals of the ornate chandelier.

While the housekeeper and plumber went upstairs, JF padded down to the basement where he knew Morgan had moved her bedroom for privacy. He passed through a laundry room and found a closed door with a sign that said *Do Not Disturb!*

He wondered if it would be locked, but when he tried the door it let out a sharp whine as it opened. So here it was: her bedroom, her woman cave.

On Morgan's bureau in a little glass dish was the silver chai necklace she'd worn every day, *chai* for life in Hebrew. Despite how troubled she was, Morgan had plenty of joie de vivre. JF gathered the pendant in his palm and then stuffed it into a pocket of his damp parka.

Her bed was covered with a quilt in pastel blues and greens and a bunch of marbles had spilled out of their black velvet pouch onto the coverlet. They were a wonder—not only cat's eyes, but also glass globes with swirls of colour, elaborate designs of flowers, and symbols and hieroglyphics that confounded him. JF hadn't known Morgan collected marbles. As he sat on the bed, marbles rolled into his thigh. He gathered them into his hands and let them fall back onto the quilt through spread fingers. Some rolled off the bed and made a hard pocking sound as they hit the concrete floor. Had she collected marbles or played games with them? Maybe with Collier? What else didn't he know about her?

JF went to Morgan's desk where he found her drawing pens and an open stiff-backed sketchbook that he leafed through page by page. It looked like she'd started to work on some sort of graphic novel or maybe a memoir. On one page, a caricaturish drawing of Morgan exaggerated her nose and the wildness of her hair. She held her hands against her ears as she walked with a figure who appeared to be Collier along the Lachine Canal. Her head was empty of facial features but contained a hunched black cat with green eyes about to spring. *Do you see it too?* she asked the Collier figure.

JF knew Morgan had suffered. He'd wanted to comfort her any way he could, as friend or lover. Would that have done any good? He'd felt helpless.

The scarf Morgan had worn in the colder months was slung over her desk chair, also in blues and greens, but with deeper hues than those on the bedspread. He buried his face in the scarf—it still had her scent, a salty-sweet mix of sweat and patchouli—and wrapped it around his neck to feel its warmth and softness.

JF sat for a while longer, hard to tell exactly how much time had passed, but eventually he heard footsteps and voices from above and crept stealthily upstairs, skulking out the front door.

BEFORE I DIE...

I want to not feel dead
I want to talk to Morgan's ghost or spirit or soul or whatever
I want to travel to Costa Rica to see those sea turtles

JF stood outside Nico's office, the door ajar. He could see that it was its usual mess of strewn toys, Chinese take-out cartons dripping greasy brown sauces, and to-go coffee containers on every possible surface.

When Nico spotted JF, he stood up from his desk to his full uncomfortably tall height, lanky and physically awkward with enormous hands and feet, large dark eyes, and long wild black hair streaked with silver that he'd pulled back into a ratty ponytail and tied with twine. He was wearing one of his loud Hawaiian shirts with a turtleneck underneath, baggy gold wide-wale cords, and fuzzy slippers. Though this was their fourth session, Nico's appearance still came as a surprise.

"Hey there! I thought you'd stood me up."

JF shrugged. "I can't. Not today."

"Well," Nico loped over to JF, patting him on the shoulder, "how about we walk and talk while we're walking."

It was a statement, not a question. Nico didn't wait for JF's answer, just suited up in his parka and boots and headed out, locking his office door.

They made their way toward La Montagne, which was not far from Nico's office. Nico had a slow, shambling gait, a bit like a character JF had seen on a rerun of a very old TV show called *The Munsters*, which his grandfather had watched with him. Nico was like Lurch, a kind of gentle giant Frankenstein.

They headed into the wooded path which was covered with black ice beneath a dusting of snow. It was nearly twilight and there were not many people around, just the occasional cross-country skier, two elderly people snowshoeing, the odd dog walker. The quiet suited JF. Now and then Nico lost his footing in a long slide, the snow obscuring the icy patches, and JF steadied his therapist so he wouldn't take a pratfall.

"Last week you were starting to talk about Morgan," Nico said in his deep voice, gritty from decades of chain smoking—he had the breath and the yellowish fingernails and teeth to prove it. "Tell me about your relationship."

They hiked uphill. "I wouldn't really call it *a relationship*." JF heard the snarl of sarcasm in his tone.

"Okay. Your connection."

"Well...." JF stopped as a flock of crows flapped overhead against the dark blue sky and he glimpsed a crescent of silver moon. "I helped Morgan with her homework now and then. We were in science class together. She panicked before exams and I was sort of like a tutor."

"How did you like that?"

JF had felt more alive when he was with Morgan. She had an intensity about her that was contagious, that shot through him, made him burn brighter too. And she was beautiful and sexy as hell with her nearly black hair that rippled and shined over her shoulders and down her back and her pale green eyes, the irises spiked with flecks of gold and blue.

"I went to her house once," JF said. "You know, to study."

It had begun to snow and Nico grabbed a toque out of his pocket and pulled it low over his forehead.

JF remembered that afternoon which had stretched out into evening. Her parents were out at some sort of gathering or meeting, he had no idea what it was. He and Morgan studied first at the dining room table, but when it got dark they went outside, bringing steaming cups of mint tea and sat in camp chairs looking up at the night sky. It was fall and the air was crisp and clean, the night extraordinarily clear. JF pointed out Aquarius, the water-bearer, and then Pegasus, the winged horse. Morgan couldn't see Pegasus, so she came over and sat in JF's lap and he put his arms around her, felt the plush firmness of her body and then took her hand in his and traced the formation of the winged horse. When she finally saw it, Morgan gave out a gleeful yelp. He could have sat there forever. Morgan came to Shabbat dinner at his house later that week.

Remembering, JF felt a rush of pleasure.

Nico, out of breath from the climb, looked over at JF. "You're smiling. What are you thinking about?" Nico breathed heavily for a few minutes, then tapped his parka. "Mind if I—?"

Again, he didn't wait for JF's okay before lighting up one of his stinky French cigarettes and inhaling deeply with a sigh of satisfaction. He held it with his fingers furled inward, facing his chest.

JF didn't want to tell Nico—or anyone for that matter—about that evening with Morgan. It was one of the few memories of them together that he cherished as his alone. That night, he'd had no idea that in a few months she'd be dead. Weird to think of that now. *It was like I loved her to death.*

Nico waited for the answer that would not come as a big fat skunk waddled across the trail, its black body and single white stripe stark against the snow. And then the creature let out his stink.

"Oh, geez," Nico said, "let's move on."

They pressed on uphill and Nico murmured, "So I sense that you did have a connection."

What? Does he read minds? Nico was staring at the blue-and-green scarf wrapped around JF's neck. Did he know that it had been Morgan's, that JF had stolen it? How could he? Impossible.

Sneaking into houses, stealing a dead girl's stuff—this was not JF's style. The only time he'd ever stolen anything was when he was five years old and took a candy bar from the front rack at the dépanneur and forgot to pay even though his moms had given him money. He'd felt so independent being allowed to walk over on his own to the corner store, but when the owner stopped him at the door and confronted him about the unpaid-for treat, he cried hysterically. The owner knew his family and called Rachel who came to get him and comforted JF until he calmed down. In truth, he'd always been a bit of a goody two-shoes. He hated himself.

They came into a clearing and while Nico stopped to catch his breath again JF looked up at the night sky. All he could see now were whirling flakes of snow dancing against the deep blue, Morgan's favourite colour. Nico had brought a water bottle and gave JF a sip, then took a long drink himself.

They continued on, walking and talking. JF felt so afraid, uncertain about what was next—next hour, next day, next week, next month, next year. Unless there was no more next.

WHAT AM I AFRAID OF?

Living more than being dead
What has been stolen
What remains

They arrived at the top of the mountain, at the lookout, the chalet behind them. Dusk brought a gauzy twilight that softened the glow of the hundreds of twinkling lights below so they furred like dandelion puffs about to gust and disperse in the winter wind. Nothing solid or stable, everything in motion.

"It should've been me," JF said, looking straight ahead. "Or maybe we could've died together."

"But you didn't." Nico's pebbly voice was firm, lower than usual.

JF's chest hurt, his heart crushed.

"The world needs you."

JF snorted at this absurd sentimental notion—he had his mom Rachel's raucous laugh that seem to come from the nose as much as the chest—and mimed the gag reflex, but coughed instead, hacking until his eyes teared, hot and stinging. He wrapped Morgan's scarf tighter around his neck and felt the sharp points and smooth curves of the chai charm shoved into his pocket, rubbing its edges, pricking his skin till he bled. They stood there for a long while until there were very few people, just a couple of dog walkers.

"For next week, I want you to write a little each day or night," Nico said. "Let's say, tonight, while you are sleeping, a miracle happens. When you wake up tomorrow, what are some of the things you notice that tell you your life has suddenly gotten better? Think about it."

Nico went into the chalet to get them both a coffee from the coin-operated machine. JF stayed put.

He found himself remembering some of the random platitudes he'd read about loss and grief in the little pamphlet the school counsellor had handed out to their whole class after Morgan's death. It had said that he had to grieve what he'd lost—truly sit with it because only then could he appreciate what he'd kept. *You must reckon with, face your own darkness.* Maybe that last one was from Oprah?

In an earlier session, Nico led JF into a discussion of his intuitions, inklings, premonitions, his sense of what was to come. "Look at your list," he said. "What needs your attention? What are you avoiding? Bad things that have happened blow up and warp our beliefs about ourselves," Nico told him. "Confront your negative beliefs. I'll share one of mine—I'm a clumsy oaf and all I'm good for is work. Now you can confront one of yours."

In family therapy, Nico had passed out M&M's, giving seven pieces each to him, his moms, and Guy. They had to sort their candy by colour. Green was for words to describe your family. Orange symbolized what you'd like to change. Red indicated what you were afraid of. Yellow was your favourite memories of your family. They each took a turn to give their responses and then picked the next person to talk.

One day Nico instructed them to breathe together for a set amount of time—ten minutes—which felt like an eternity. He asked them to breathe at least two dozen deep, slow breaths in sync with one another.

The activities they did, like his writing assignments, seemed lame and cheesy at first, but despite that his moms, Guy, and even JF got into it. What else could they do? His moms wouldn't let up, they would not quit. At some family meetings, the four of them had ugly fights where they cried and screamed at each other. But somehow after these devastating sessions, JF felt a kind of release, a calm and cleansing exhaustion that soothed him, like the sound of the train clattering by on the tracks near their apartment, regular as clockwork, almost like a friend during these long days and endless nights.

JF kept his appointments with Nico, one of the few constants in his life now, a regular window of time that gave a shape to the void he felt himself in, the void that was him.

He was looking forward to that steaming cup of coffee, to holding it between his hands, against his chest. So he had another writing assignment. His final line wasn't written; whenever wasn't here yet. Today wouldn't come again.

JF and Nico would wind their way down and around the mountain until they got to the bottom, out of the woods, and into the street. He'd go home. Maybe there'd be pizza. His moms were waiting for him.

SHIVAH

Rachel

FIRST DAY

A pitcher of water perches outside our door. Inside, the stout shivah candle burns bright, its glass canister adorned with the Star of David. The mirrors are covered. The shivah callers all stand around balancing plates of food, talking about me, and sharing memories. Natalie and Guy each wear a torn black ribbon pinned to their sombre clothes. I scan the crowd crammed into the small living room in the apartment I shared with Natalie. Our son JF is nowhere in sight.

I count the bodies one by one. Twenty-four in all. Not bad for a first day.

A clique gathers around the silent piano. I'm the one who played—classical, jazz, showtunes, you name it. Sitting at the piano and banging out some music, no matter how it sounded, helped me unwind after an intense day on the children's ward. Sometimes Guy and JF accompanied me on guitar and Nat sang, our little quartet. Natalie has a beautiful voice and I always wished she'd do more with her talent, but she just sang for pleasure. Anyway, who has time to do more with anything? Me. Time is all I have. All of time.

Cody is talking about my first day on the children's psych ward, about how a young girl suffering a first episode psychosis kept tugging my "flaming red hair," convinced it was a wig. A wig on fire. (I did try out a red wig, once; it was a day neither Natalie nor

I will ever forget.) Stavros remembers a costume party I organized for the kids at Halloween during my second year on the job. Our craft project was making masks to depict joys, fears, sorrows. It was risky, but it was such a relief for most of the kids to let their imaginations roam wild in papier mâché and to dress up their fantasies in polyester. The masks and costumes each kid created told me more about them than hours of talk. I remember shopping in craft shops and at Renaissance to fill that dress-up box, putting myself into the skin of each and every kid on the ward. I loved that job from the first day, even when I had a tough time, even when a kid broke my heart.

Wait a minute. Is Stavros actually saying someone is coming in next week for the position of recreation therapist? *My* job? I can't hang around; it's too painful. That life goes on.

Where is Natalie? I scan the room and then drift over to the alcove I used as an office or just as a place for alone time when I needed to collect myself after work or when I was overwhelmed by JF's pain, by the fact that as his mom I couldn't take it away and claim it for my own. There's Natalie sitting in my mustard-coloured armchair, her feet flat, hands folded, her face cold and blank and empty. I've never seen her sit like this, so prim. Death does strange things to people.

After a while, Guy finds her. There's barely room for the two of them in the alcove, especially with my big cushiony armchair. That's kind of what I loved about that place, a room of one's own with room for one only, my little hollow.

I want to put my arms around Natalie, I long to whisper in her ear.

This first day is long, as Natalie followed my wishes to the letter. I hover around for Rabbi Avram's prayer.

Finally, the apartment is empty of shivah callers and I place a pair of buttermints on Nat's pillow, the last two from our final stash. The meltaways are pale pink and mint green, candy kiss shaped and crusted with white sprinkles, Nat's fav. We made a special trip to buy them before I got sick, an outing to walk along Lake Champlain and visit the general store in North Hero, Vermont, where they stock all kinds of old-fashioned, hard-to-find sweets and treats. I scrawl out a note on the little pad with pen attached that Natalie keeps by her bedside, in case she thinks of something to add to her to-dos while tossing and turning with insomnia.

'Night, my love.

Natalie

SECOND DAY

I wake up with the creamy sweet film of mint meltaways still on my tongue and tuck the note into my cleavage with a deranged little chuckle. *Get a cat!* Well, maybe I will *now*. *Finalement*. Rachel didn't like cats, claimed she was allergic, but she knew how much I wanted a kitty. Now is the time. If not now, when? *Shit!* She wrote it on my to-do list. I'd recognize that handwriting anywhere with the old-fashioned *a*'s and the *t* which inexplicably has a tail like a *j*. I know it's possible that she prepared this little surprise for me with the help of the home hospice nurse before she died. The nurse stopped by late yesterday to pick up some things she'd left behind. I like to think, though, that it's Rachel, that she's still here in some form, looking out for us.

Yesterday, after the burial and during the long hours of the first day of the shivah, I felt an exhaustion like I've never experienced in my life. Even on my longest shifts at the hospital in the oncology ward; even after the crisis with JF when he blamed himself for the death of his friend, Morgan; even after we lost my beloved dad when I was a teenager.

I've been caring for Rachel at home the past few months and she died in her own bed as she wanted to do. I didn't take any breaks and needed to make sure she was comfortable and said everything she had to say.

It was a lot! Rachel got very Type A toward the end, super bossy. I had to take notes.

But I got that. When you can't control your body anymore, you desperately need to have agency over *something*. And this was important stuff. She wanted a traditional Jewish funeral and burial *and* a customary shivah in our home—all seven days—the whole *megillah*.

About five years before, we'd joined the only Reconstructionist synagogue in Montreal, a place with artists, intellectuals, and progressive thinkers that welcomed LGBTQ people, where women also read from the Torah.

Personally, I was raised Catholic, like Guy, and still consider myself a Catholic. I never converted to Judaism and Rachel was okay with that decision. In fact, raising JF, we celebrated both Jewish and Catholic holidays, which is saying a lot because there always seemed to be a Jewish holiday coming around the corner or just ending and a few of them last for eight days, and then add in the Catholic festivities. We were always celebrating *something*.

Honestly, there are things I like about both faiths. I know it sounds weird, but I'm addicted to confession, it helps me, the ritual cleansing. I pray with the rosary and I love the feel of the cool hard smoothness of the beads in my hands. And I would never give up Christmas, especially midnight Mass and eggnog in front of the fire, not to mention Easter and church and egg hunts. Yet I love Judaism's warmth, the healthy attitude toward sexuality, and Jewish food, which is just about the best in the world. I don't know what I'd do without *latkes* and *matzoh brei* and *kugel*. Hell, I'm one of the last holdouts for chopped liver on rye. And then there's the sound of Yiddish and Hebrew! I listened at services and watched *Shtisel* and *Prisoners of War* and managed to pick up a sprinkling of words and expressions without even trying. Like *beseder*, which sounds like what it means—okay—a comforting word. And *toda sheba 'atem*, thanks for coming today. I'll be saying that a lot this week. *Schmear* is Yiddish for the whole works and sometimes at Fairmount Bagel someone will ask for a bagel with a *schmear*. *Shoyn genug* means that's enough! These expressions come in handy. I'm still learning.

Rachel and I went to the Shul for community. It was a welcoming place. Mind you, we didn't get to actual Shabbat services all that often, but we did other things. We took courses in Yiddish literature and belly dancing; we went to dinners called the Enlightened Bite, gourmet vegan meals with a short talk usually by the rabbi on a part of the Torah or Jewish culture. We went on outings, such as a guided walk around Old Jewish Montreal with plenty of history and noshing. I might take another class at the Shul once I get back on my feet, learn more Yiddish maybe. I loved our Friday night Shabbat dinners at home, sometimes JF brought a friend along. Now I'll have to continue that ritual on my own.

Rabbi Avram Rappaport met with the two of us a number of times at our home when it was clear that Rachel would not get through this third bout of breast cancer. She was only forty-four years old. And JF just eighteen. Why why why why do some awful people live to one hundred? Billy Joel got it right: only the good die young.

Rabbi Avram taught me about the stages of mourning in Judaism. There are five which correspond to the stages of the soul's ascent.

I learned that *shivah* means seven and comes from the Hebrew word *shiv'ah*. It took seven days to create the world. When creation is reversed and the soul returns to its source, this too, is marked with a week's cycle.

At the end of the first day, I spoke to the rabbi and found out that I could designate hours for shivah visits and didn't need to be "on call," so to speak, all day and all evening. What a relief! Guy got word around that we would be taking shivah calls from ten o'clock in the morning until noon, and again from four to six in the afternoon. If I wanted to stay in bed for the rest of the day or zone out in a fugue state, that was up to me.

I had to realize that I wasn't a hostess here. My role was not to take care of the guests. It was a time to grieve and be comforted, but I didn't know if I could grieve and be comforted on demand, in a group, with people floating in and out of our apartment, the same place Rachel had suffered and died.

As if I too had risen both out of my own body and emotions, hard to feel anything at all. Numb and waiting for fingertips and toes to tingle.

JF stood in the back at the funeral and came and went from the burial before I had a chance to hug him. He still hasn't shown up at the shivah.

Most of this second day I stay in bed. Guy took care of everything. Before he left, I was about to ask him and he shook his head. He knew what I was going to say before the words came out of my mouth. "He's hurting," Guy said. "He'll get here."

Before I return to bed, I find some wine gums that are not yet past their sell-by date and place a few on Rachel's pillow. I feel a little lighter, mischievous. Two can play at this game. I scrawl out a note of my own: *I will get a cat.* Feeling silly or concerned that I'm losing my mind—at last—I throw out the candy and tear up the note, not wanting to find them there in the morning. Then I go back to bed and sleep a deep and velvety sleep.

JF

THIRD DAY

I walk and keep walking. Maybe if I keep moving, Mom will be alive. Maybe if I'd never been born, Mom never would've gotten breast cancer. (But then I wouldn't exist.) Maybe if I hadn't brought Oxy to Morgan's birthday party, she would've seen eighteen. I can't stop these thoughts circling round and around.

I keep my head down, avoid eye contact. The fall day beats down on me in its beauty, the leaves scarlet, gold, and orange, piles of them to swish and crunch through in the gutter, Mom's favourite season.

I can't go back to the apartment, not now, not yet, lousy with shivah callers helping us grieve, mourning together. Yikes! My dad's there to help Mom, so I'm not really needed at the moment.

From behind, I feel a tap on my shoulder and jump. An older man dressed in layers and an unravelling olive toque, bald but for a few silvery wild wisps blowing in the wind, is talking to me.

"Where the hell's the food dep?"

I look around, realize I'm on Marlowe, at the border of NDG and Westmount in front of an old church. "I have no clue."

"Used to be right here." He points to the church, his hands in grey cut-off woolly mittens, his fingers bare.

I slip my phone out of my pocket and Google it. "Looks like they're on Somerled now."

"Since when?"

"Dunno."

"That's a ways."

"Not too bad by bus."

"Don't have my OPUS."

"I'll take you over," I say, desperate for something to do other than go home. It'll be a *mitzvah*, helping someone, even if it isn't the person I'm supposed to be helping now.

I take his arm, and we walk to Vendôme, where we wait for a while, not talking much, before getting on the bus to the NDG food depot. When we arrive, they're serving lunch to a bunch of families and other folks. Two young women about my age ladle out bowls of chili and cut big wedges of cornbread. One's tall and pretty with delicate features, the other one short and heavily muscled with a shaved head. The food smells delicious and I realize I haven't eaten all day.

"Joe!" the tall slender woman calls out; she's wearing cool red-framed glasses, and her hair is in small braids adorned with different coloured beads, which clack as she moves. "Haven't seen you in a while. How you been?"

"Travelling," he says, lining up.

I stop into the washroom. I'm on my way out when Joe intercepts me holding a bowl of chili.

"Oh, no need."

"Take a load off," he coaxes.

I glance toward the door, then back inside. I would do anything to delay going back home. Taking the bowl of chili, I follow Joe back to the dining area and take a seat on a long bench.

"You're a good boy," he says, patting me so hard on the back that chili sloshes over my spoon onto the table; Joe swabs it up with a triangle of paper towel.

"So where you been travelling?" I ask, making conversation, not my strong suit.

"In time," he says, matter-of-factly, taking a glug of his water.

"Oh yeah?"

"Into the past and onto the future and back again."

"Wow." I realize I've been doing some time travelling myself. Obsessing over the past, anxious about the future. McGill accepted me for this fall, but I couldn't bring myself to start with Mom so sick. Haven't figured out what to do next. Or even now.

I like the people in the food depot, and after I finish lunch, I chat with the slim woman who's been so friendly to Joe. Maybe I could work here. I'd be doing some good.

Maureen, that's her name, points me toward the director, Starr, and I fill out an application in a small office in the back. "I could volunteer till a position comes through," I add on my way out. I'll get a second job, something mindless, at the IGA or maybe as an Uber Eats delivery man. Uber Eats is huge in town, in every season, any time of day. I've got a bike.

Before saying goodbye to Joe, I ask him about a men's shelter, just in case. He pulls a matchbook from his shirt pocket and scrawls the details on its inside cover.

I tromp around the city all afternoon and into the evening. Before I go to the shelter, I text my mom.

Staying with a friend. Hope the shiver is going ok.

Autocorrect triumphs again. I figure I'll return home once this grieving circus is over and done with. Four more days. And then what?

Rachel

FOURTH DAY

What is it about our culture? Valuing the end of life more than its quality. I'm not tragic, no. With death I'm in an eternal present.

Playing jacks with Nat, grade one.

Passing to Nat on the soccer field, Nat kicking into the goal. I'm left-winger and she is centre forward, stars of our team.

Nat reading aloud to me near the end from some of my favourite books from way back when: *A Wrinkle in Time, The Secret Garden, The Phantom Tollbooth*.... All journeys, I realize, at the end of my own. How I've hated that word, but now I've softened toward it.

JF confiding in me about his love for Morgan.

Doing one of my kickboxing moves to jostle the vending machine at the children's ward and free up Nat's three favourite snack choices for her night shift.

Talking with Collier Sampson on the roof in summer after that wigged-out aunt of theirs started a fire in the washroom.

Seeing that shrink about JF, sporting the red wig, yanking it off. Oh, the look on her face!

Family meetings with Nico that broke us down and put us back together.

Low back pain so bad I couldn't sit down, my normally clear thoughts addled like a jumble of mashed-up ingredients in the blender. Cancer, round three—and you're out!

Natalie

FIFTH DAY

The first thing I see when I open my eyes is the bright rectangle of my phone open to the "Cats for Adoption" page on the SPCA website. I don't remember Googling it last night, though it was on my to-dos. I bring two cups of coffee into our bedroom, mine with cream and sugar, Rachel's black in her favourite blue cracked mug. I'm the morning person and bringing her a coffee to wake up is just something I do. When I realize my mistake I dash into the kitchen and drain her mug in the sink.

Over my own coffee, I scroll through photos of gorgeous kitties needing homes and note adoption hours Monday through Sunday.

Somehow, someway, I make it through this quiet day, the shivah callers trickling down to just a few. I'm less exhausted since I determined specific visiting hours, just saying. There are regulars: Rabbi Avram, of course, who passes by each day for prayers; Cody, who can't keep away; as well as a woman I don't recognize but overhear is the mom of one of the kids Rachel worked with at the children's ward. Many were grateful for her care at possibly the worst time in their lives as parents.

Haven't been able to cry since Rachel's death. Not at the funeral, not at the burial, not at the shivah.

Holding Rachel's hand near the end, I sang the *Shema* and tears streamed down her cheeks and mine; we cried together. *Shema* means listen or hear. She was alive, then.

Her death is not real to me. She hovers, a presence. I can't let her go. I'm having conversations with her and don't know how to stop.

Midway through the late afternoon shivah, I ask Rabbi Avram if I can have a moment. We seclude ourselves in the alcove Rachel used as an office. I don't have a so-called room of my own; I haven't felt the need for one, or maybe I just wanted Rach to have that little extra space to herself in our modest apartment.

"I still feel like I'm failing, that I'm supposed to be some sort of lady of the house or something."

Rabbi Avram smiles with his eyes more than his mouth. Standing awkwardly in the cozy space, I'm clumsy and out of sorts.

"Do you want to sit down, Natalie?" he asks, pointing to Rachel's big armchair, but then there would be no place for him unless he sits in my lap!

Rabbi Avram is handsome, tall, and lanky with silky black hair that waves thickly over his collar, dark, long-lashed eyes, and graceful hands. He has a gorgeous singing voice and plays guitar. The man isn't yet forty.

I perch on one arm of the chair. "I don't know," I say. "It's as if time has stopped. No, that's not what I mean, more like it's flowing and things that happened ages ago I'm not remembering, but experiencing *now*. Being there, here, it's all collapsed, past present future."

I can't imagine going on without Rachel. She's always been here, a part of my life, going back to when we were very young children. My life is unnatural without her. It's like I've lost a limb, but can still feel its phantom tingling. And this is just the beginning. There will be days and weeks and months and years to get through, as I am, as Rachel put it, "disgustingly healthy." Disgusting, indeed.

"You know JF's gotten into McGill," I say.

"That's wonderful," Rabbi Avram replies. "Mazel tov." To my surprise, he sits on the other arm of the chair, his long legs stretched out before him.

"But he's not starting this fall. With Rachel being sick—I mean, you know...."

And then the tears come. I'm loud and my nose runs and drips onto my lovely black dress; I don't have a tissue. Rabbi Avram is quiet, just there. He gives me a handkerchief from his pocket and puts his hand on my shaking forearm, the tiniest pressure that's a comfort.

Amazing to think, he doesn't need to say—anything.

JF

SIXTH DAY

I keep away from the shivah though Mom knows I'm all right— well, if not okay, alive, anyway, crashing at a friend's place. I wear myself out tramping around the city until I can't think or feel except for one foot in front of the other, blisters on my heels and between my toes, knees aching. I've run through my old sneakers and have a used pair from the men's shelter that are too small for my big feet. Doesn't stop me. I need to walk to sort myself out, a habit I've gotten into with Nico, whose voice is in my head.

The Jewish guilt thing never stops. And I'm not even totally one hundred percent Jewish, but there's Catholic guilt too. I don't know how much all of our therapy helped—family sessions, group sessions for me with kids my age, and private sessions. I understand more about myself and I loved and sometimes hated Nico Tesoro, but it didn't take away the pain. "Who the hell says," Nico bellowed one day, "that we're supposed to be happy? Happy is not what life's about!" Tell me about it. That shook me straight. I miss Nico. He was, is, an original.

In some ways I've had a charmed childhood. I hit the jackpot having two moms and they are, I mean *were,* so good together. Truly complementary. Nom was the brass tacks, pragmatic disciplinarian, and Rom was full of games and fun, up for anything, anytime, anywhere. Though she had her serious side, working in the children's psych ward and knowing she was only a few steps ahead of breast cancer.

I spent time with her towards the end before she was too ill to talk. At that point, I traced out words and sentences on her forearm, and she listened and wrote back on the veiny inside of my arm. Both my moms were so happy about me getting into McGill. I told Rom I didn't know if I could go, what I'd study, or what I wanted to do or be.

You'll figure it out, she traced out on my arm. *I believe in you, JF!* Her message took a while, and then she squeezed my hand hard, I was surprised by the strength of her grip.

My dad's been trying to make up for lost time, straining to be more in my life. For a while I didn't even consider him my dad—he was such a distant figure, gone away for so long.

Both my moms asked me to try and let him in.

Where will you go? I asked my mom near the end, tracing my question onto the inside of her pale soft forearm and wrist. I meant where would she be buried. I knew that she wanted to be buried in the ground as per traditional Jewish law, but I wasn't sure where our plot was or if we had one, being half Catholic and half Jewish.

She traced out her answer on my forearm: *Eternal Gardens.*

And then she lifted her pale soft arms from the bedsheets, cradled my head in her hands, and coaxed me to lie down beside her. There was room.

Rachel

SEVENTH DAY

Oh, my. There's a big crowd on the last day of the shivah, forty-one and counting, spread out throughout our ground floor, some spilling over onto the porch. Fall is drawing in; IT is coming, our unrelenting six-month winter. I can feel it in the autumn sunshine, which is glassy rather than warm, and in the chill on the underside of every breeze that blows the flaming leaves in airborne wreaths. This gorgeous weather is an expectation, possibility, more than dread.

The memories and reminiscences and mythologies are coming fast and furiously. My older brother, Morris, is telling the story about how in preschool, during naptime, I put on my boots and snowsuit and snuck outside into a blizzard, sledding down the big hill at Beaver Lake on a stiff piece of cardboard I'd found lying around. My mom chimes in that they wanted to kick me out of the preschool, expel me, because they couldn't be responsible, even though it was the teachers who were literally out to lunch.

Natalie is up and dressed, looking pretty in a midnight-blue shift that shows off her curves and she's telling everyone how I saved up ABC gum in grade six, stockpiling it, so I could write a message to her on the bottom of my desk in blisters of gum that she read like braille when she borrowed scissors from me.

"What did she write?" Stavros asks.

"Going to the moon," Natalie says matter-of-factly.

That was our code for sneaking off to La Montagne after school and climbing up to the top, where we'd use our lunch money to buy hot chocolate and cookies at the Chalet snack bar, munching away while taking in the aerial view of the city.

And then someone launches through the open door, staring at and then touching the *mezuzah* in the frame and then lightly kissing their fingertips. Though it's been two years, I recognize them right away: Collier Sampson. Collier looks well, their hair still long and shiny pale, dressed in a black belted jumpsuit and booties, looking around at everyone with those startling seaglass eyes. And right after them, finally, at last, in walks JF.

Seeing JF and Collier together, well, it's almost too much for me. I want them to connect, to be friends; they have so much in common, really, losing both Morgan and their moms.

JF says hello to Collier and then, rather hostile, demands to know, "What are *you* doing here?"

Collier stands up straighter. They weren't going to take any shit, not from JF. "She saved my life, your mom."

Everyone stops their chatter and looks at Collier.

JF opens the top two buttons of his shirt, as if he's too hot or constrained by the collar. Collier stares at him.

"Where did you get Morgan's chai?"

I remember when I first noticed the necklace and asked JF about it. He told me that it was Morgan's and I left it at that; I had more pressing concerns on my mind.

JF's hand flies to his throat and he holds the charm between his thumb and forefinger. "I'm fucked up." In a moment JF unclasps the necklace, and walking behind Collier, fastens it around their neck. "I'm sure she would've wanted you to have it."

Collier slowly closes their eyes for a moment.

JF shakes his head. "I can't believe she's gone."

"It's been two years," Collier says softly, "but I know what you mean."

"No, I mean my mom. I can't believe *she's* gone. *Where?*"

Then was now and now was then and now. Time swirls a gorgeous pinwheel of colour.

I'm here. I'm there. I circle my ghostly hands, palms down, as I did each Friday night over the Shabbat candles before saying the prayer. *Everywhere.*

AURORA

Collier

Did you jump or fall? Fall or jump, jump or fall?

When I get like this, I can't do anything but pace back and forth. I tell myself I will head out to the grocery store for milk, I say it over and over to myself like a mantra, seeing the black words on the white screen of my mind tick out like the sound of an old grandfather clock, over and over but the other words inside my head won't let me go.

I don't want to end up back in the psych ward, and this time around, it won't be the gentle care I got at the Children's Hospital. How did I get to be twenty-six?

Come back here. Be in this place.

Here I am. Yeah, it's taken me ten years to get back to this house, which was our home, and this treehouse, our haven. Not that I haven't been thinking of you, about whether I could've saved you.

Early this morning, I was wandering the old neighbourhood and saw the family who lives in our old place packing up their battered van. Kept my head down to avoid any unwanted attention in my jean mini-skirt, white tank, Morgan's chai necklace which I never take off, Pepto-pink high-tops, and long blonde wig with its perfect bangs. I'm practised by now, going about my business and ignoring the stares and comments.

It was fairly easy to get in by climbing the wooden fence and bushwhacking through the hedge. I'm agile in a skirt. Everything is in better shape than it was when we lived here and there's this heady smell of honeysuckle. The lawn is cropped and green. Dad never had much luck with our grass, which was rife with dandelions and baby maples, and pocked with bald patches. Not that *we* cared.

Our minds were on loftier things: chatting, planning, singing, dancing, imagining all the things we would do… someday. I know you had dreams you never went after. Your big one was to sing in nightclubs around Montreal and you had a voice. Deep and grainy, like stream water through sand, your sadness seeping inside every blues note.

I climb up the wooden ladder to the treehouse. It's improved now with safety features. The steps are sturdy and there's a redwood railing that'll prevent falls. Maybe Dad meant to build a railing. Up here I feel the work of his hands standing up to time and the assault of Montreal winters. It's a beautiful treehouse with a real door, two large windows, and a view out over the neighbourhood. I love the feeling of being above the petty world, seeing but not being seen. A neighbour has put in a swimming pool and another has a trampoline. The city is lush now that it's summer, a gentle wind ruffling the flowers and leaves.

As a kid, I used to love Montreal summers, but all these years later I feel a sense of impending doom when the days warm and lengthen and the trees leaf out and bloom.

On bad days, nights, I get a thought and it spools out over and over, expanding, taking up all the space in my mind, heart, and soul.

A bird crashes into the ledge of one of the treehouse windows. It's a black mangy thing with crumpled wings, bent beak, and crusts in its eyes. Aurora, dear mother? You've flown back to me.

Darling, I should have broken a leg or an arm, but I hit my head on a big ass rock and died instantly. I want you to know that I felt no pain.

Can I touch you?

Your head nods three times.

I stroke your throat, which has a patch of dirty pink feathers; they tremble under my touch. We are together again.

I love to be stroked on my gorget. It's usually only in male birds, but I'm special.

Stroking, rubbing rhythmically, that day comes back to me.

I see us dancing, whirling to our Motown tunes. You spin, once, twice, three times, each twirl edging closer to the ledge, and then you are pirouetting midair. I watch you plummet, hear a thud and a crack as your head hits rock and your body crumples. Your ballet skirt is flung backward over your torso, your pale legs and black panties exposed.

I need to cover you. But I'm up here.

If only I'd been down below, I could've caught you, broken your fall.

Afterward Dad and I were hauled down to the police station and interrogated. They were not kind, police people rarely are—to me—being a man and a woman and neither and both. Made all sorts of cracks behind my back loud enough for me to hear. Stuff about a chick with a dick and a dick with a trick. There was a social worker from family services and she sat with me while they grilled Dad. I still remember her name, Grace, and that she had kind eyes as she offered me a glass of juice and a shortbread biscuit, afraid I might faint like people can after giving blood.

I know Dad had some sketchy dealings in his past and problems paying back taxes. I tell myself this explains why he took off and left me. Not a word all these years.

You flap about the treehouse, ledge to ledge, beating grungy wings, your broken beak tapping the ceiling. How much I've missed this place.

Maybe one day I'll hear from my dad—who knows? I don't fret about it anymore with everything going on in my life. It used to bother me how uncomfortable I made him, being fluid. His shame erased me. But I had you.

You flap about, fluttering your scuzzy wings. I wonder where you've been and where you are going.

What happened? I need to know, to understand.

We were dancing.

We loved Motown—Marvin Gaye, Aretha, Oleta, The Temps. It was the Four Tops playing that day, one of our faves, "You

Keep Running Away"! Too apt, I think. Now if that song's playing any*time,* any*where,* I break back into that moment.

You thud onto my wrist, making it dip, and look at me with your scrofulous eyes. I flick a yellow crust from your lid.

I was such a young mother, sixteen, and didn't know who I was or where I belonged in the world. Who does? But I knew I wanted you. They told me I was having a boy. I would have been happy with a boy or a girl and I got both! I never thought about whether I would keep you, just how we'd survive.

You *didn't.*

Offended, you flap away from me and perch on a lilac branch. Soon you are back inside the treehouse on the window ledge.

I loved having a young mom. We were more like sibs.

We lived with my parents when you were little. 'Member?

Just that Pops used to fold his eyelids up to scare me! He had a ginger beard and stank of cigars, and his fingernails were yellow. Nana was a big lady who wore cotton tents scattered with flowers and old slippers because her feet swelled; she had bunions. I don't remember how or when they died. Just that they stopped being around.

I didn't know death.

You fly up toward the treehouse roof and then flutter to the guardrail, perching there. I follow you.

When I was a teenager, before you were born, I worked cleaning houses. Had a big ring of keys for my regulars, made me feel like somebody. I didn't mind it too much, but it was hard on my back and knees and my hands were rubbed raw from cleaning products. I liked being inside all those homes, places I would never get to see, other worlds.

Often the house was empty while I worked. I loved examining what was in the fridge, flipping through closets, checking drawers and bathroom cabinets. You could learn a lot about people from their stuff like the fact that your best friend's father, Joshua Rosenblum, ate Werther's by the package while he was composing and his wife Delia wrote out little wish lists that she tore into pieces.

I always made Joshua squeamish or something. He was awkward around me and yet took to staring as if he was riffling through a lost and found for some possession of his that'd gone missing. When I met Joshua I was sixteen.

My age when you died.

If Joshua was at the piano while I was cleaning, I'd lollygag around, going over the same shelf with the dust rag again and again just to listen. He had magic hands.

He was hardly around when I hung out with Morgan.

One day in summer we got talking. I told him about my singing and he asked me to do a song for him. I was way shy and had no confidence, but I wanted to sing for him, for someone so musical is all.

I thought it was just the two of us who did songs.

Collier, I sang my heart out for Joshua that day and he accompanied me on piano, which was a first—pure joy. My song was about a bird I saw in a vision with my very own name: Aurora. I am her now. Joshua helped me with the melody.

You settle on my wrist and the two of us go back inside the treehouse sitting on a bench built into its southern wall. Another improvement from the "new" people.

I stand up, go to the wraparound porch and lean on the guardrail, the white sun beating down on me like a maniac.

"Hey! You! What you doing up there?"

I look down, shielding my eyes with a nail-bitten hand. There is an old weather-beaten man in a soiled undershirt and patched jeans standing on the deck of the house. "I'm looking after this place!"

Fear makes me shiver despite the heat. He's on the ground and I'm up a fucking tree with no place but down.

The man approaches the treehouse. "Get!" He makes a dismissive motion with a skinny arm as though waving away a noisome pest. "Or I'll call the police." He reaches into his pocket and pulls out his phone, punching buttons.

As he gets closer, I spot the large tattoo on his forearm, a figure-eight, and remember he's my dad's old beer buddy, Lyle Stafford, also a carpenter and fix-up guy. They did some jobs together, Lyle & Logan, Logan & Lyle.

"Lyle, it's Collier, Collier Sampson." My voice comes out thin as thread.

With unexpected agility and speed, he climbs up the ladder and joins me inside the treehouse. I'm still scared and back away as much as I can without falling.

When he sees me up close, he gasps, "Whoa! Jesus, fuck, fuck Jesus."

All this time you dart around. I don't know if you're watching us. Or listening.

Lyle and I look each other up and down. My eyes fix on that infinity tattoo on his forearm. It's always intrigued me, hinting at depths I didn't know Lyle possessed, and he drinks me in like a wine you taste and nearly spit out because it's gone bad.

"So you're a girl now. I remember that time you tried on Maureen's pink cardigan, the one with the pearl buttons? And danced around all happy as pie."

"Tell me about my dad."

"Oh, Col," Lyle says, laying a leathery, gnarled hand on my shoulder. "Logan passed."

I feel an iron fist press down on my chest but can't escape being annoyed by the euphemism. Passed? Passed where? If people pass you can still catch up with them. "When?"

"Few years now. His liver went—cirrhosis. He was on a list to get a transplant. Number didn't come up."

"Did I? Come up?"

"He had no idea where you were, Collier. He was broken after your mom—well...."

"Where was he living?"

"NDG."

The hurt I feel is all too familiar, and despite the heat I'm still shivering—no sunlight, no, not for me. I fold my arms across my chest, trying to get warm again.

Lyle shakes his head, plays with his ratty ponytail. "You okay, Col?"

Aurora is back, nestling in the space between my crossed arms. I look at Lyle, see clearly that he does not see you. I want more time alone here, more time with you.

"I needed to come back here."

Lyle nods slowly. "I get that, my boy."

I let the *boy* pass. "Could I have a moment? I'll leave soon."

"No prob. Need to take care of some things around the place."

Lyle climbs down, spends a bit of time watering the flowers and lawn, then heads out.

That day, up here, we were happy. Singing and dancing and going a little crazy together with our Motown playlist and our original songs.

Your rough dirty feathers brush my chin.

That day was my window. I'd been in the tunnel for so long—dark, dank, no air, no light. But that day with you, my darling Collier, I was pure happiness. A moment. I had to hold on to it.

Don't go.

You stroke my eyes, cheeks, lips with your feathers, then fly out the window, becoming earth and sky.

THE
SLEEP *of*
APPLES

Miri

I

Just eight months ago, cold hard white crunched under my feet as I entered the *sanctuaire* of Cornucopie. I cruised down the brightly lit aisles leaning on my cart, my satchel mashed into the front compartment, wanting to taste and touch everything in those candy-coloured aisles, not to think. Picking up a grapefruit, I inhaled citrus with a hint of bitter. A candied pecan tasted dense and chewy, with a touch of salt and melt of maple. Now that I had no one to feed but myself, I enjoyed shopping. I'd had a long day with patients and their voices reverberated in my ears. I dug the Lucite shovel into the nut bin, filling one small bag, then another, craving a cigarette and a scotch. We'd share both and more in the months to come. The butcher handed me a neat packet of sirloin wrapped in waxed paper. My usual. You see, I was such a creature of habit until you shook me up.

"How's it going, Dr. Gildener?"

"Medium." I cleared my throat once, twice, a tic that unnerved me as I could not will it to stop and never knew when it would come. One of my most challenging patients had made a remark about it, diverting attention from the hard work ahead to analyze her analyst.

You were kind or polite enough never to comment.

Consulting my list, I ignored it, loading up on sweet treats, a pint of Häagen-Dazs coffee ice cream, and a Belgian chocolate bar.

When Max and Arabella were little, we had upside-down suppers on Friday nights, our own personal Shabbat dinner complete with prayers and white candles. Bella and Max racing through these aisles grabbing treats, Max's sweet laughter bubbling below Bella's excited shrieks, her thick, wild hair flying in all directions.

As I reached for a can of tomato soup, I dislodged a towering stack. I was surprised to find your arm about my waist, whisking me out of the way, and I slid smooth and swift as a chess piece, while an avalanche of canned soups tumbled down, rolling onto the floor.

"You okay?" You stood beside me in a green apron.

"I'm dying."

You looked at me with clear grey eyes.

"Been there."

I felt a leap in my belly, a knot pulled tight. Novel to look into the eyes of another grown-up without distraction, embarrassment or reserve, intimate as touch. But you did. That's what I noticed first. You stooped to gather cans of soup, your hand grazing the inside of my wrist, as I bent to help.

"Lost something?" You picked up my necklace with its two charms glimmering gold on the shiny floor. How observant you were, while I was preoccupied.

"Oh! I never take that off." My father's medical school key— NYU—and a filigreed charm, designed by Levin, my late partner, out of our entwined initials.

"Looks like a link opened. I might be able to do something."

You disappeared into the back as I waited, consulting the long list of messages on my phone. Looking around, I noticed everyone else in the market also had heads bent to small bright rectangles, fingers scrolling. Made me sad.

Five minutes later, you reappeared and stood behind me, refastening the necklace around my throat.

"Thanks so much."

You glanced into my cart. "Nothing green."

A bit cheeky—I liked that.

"Steak and chocolate, perfect." You turned and made your way down the aisle without glancing back. I watched you and noticed your strong build and athletic shoulders, your left leg dragging behind the right, the left foot turned outward.

Inside my apartment on Tupper, I set the brown paper sack on the counter and shucked off my winter layers. The sudden heat, nearly sentient, enveloped me, and I sighed with pleasure.

As I put away groceries, I thought. Who *are* you? About me, not you. What a thing I'd said. Well, it just popped out. My mother's voice inside my head, sidling up, berating, insistent as breath. *Always saying something. A bid for attention? Flirt. Fool.* If only I could shut her up, but her voice had become my own.

Night came quickly. As I lay in bed, snow fell lightly, delicate flakes translucent and glittering. So it had gotten warm enough to snow. Again. I slept well when it was snowing, the white whirl a balm from festering thoughts that chased each other in a kind of delirium. My mother hovered. Slim and elegant, Florence had rarely touched me, even when I was a child, so each isolated kiss or embrace stood out starkly. Night snows had made Mom happy, calmed her temper. We had that in common, soothed by snow.

I remember a blizzard that started after I'd been tucked into bed. I was maybe five, so excited by the white fluttering I crept downstairs and snuck onto the stoop in my bare feet. My mother must have heard me. She stood in the gold-lit doorway, her face softening.

Get back in here, Munchkin! She stepped toward me, her arms outstretched.

The snow was white butterflies. I scooped some into my hand and then my mouth with a cold, melting chill.

Come inside, Miri. You'll get sick. She was smiling. *Now, my love.*

I could feel that she wanted to join me in the whirling white darkness. I don't remember her ever calling me *my love* again.

With my own kids, we had a tradition. On the first snow each year we'd run up and down our driveway—in bare feet—shovelling fresh snow into a bucket, which I scooped into bowls and served with warmed maple syrup.

Lying awake in bed, all at once I saw your grey gaze, so like my father's. He'd sat on the edge of my bed each night until I fell asleep; he loved to cuddle and kibitz, and I was happiest with my head resting against his chest. I felt safe, so safe. More than anything, I wanted to be like him, devoted to healing, the easing of suffering. Medicine, psychiatry had always felt like my calling, as much as a profession. I had Dad to thank for that. With his eyes and yours watching over me, the snow melted into sea and I broke its surface, plunging deep into the dark watery world, my eyes open to its secrets.

II

It was exactly one week after we met. I lay shivering under a sheet awaiting surgery. My nurse, young, male, and smiling, had eyes cold as crystal. I wished you were the one I was going to wake up to, but I hardly knew you then. You later told me that you wanted to know about everything I'd been through. After your accident, you were so broken you had to start again from the beginning if you wanted to live, as if you'd experienced a painful metamorphosis— new bones, new blood, new skin. I was hoping for such a rebirth, however painful.

Lying on that table, I was angry and about to cry, fury and tears all mixed up. "Is something funny?"

"Sorry." The nurse smiled again, lips closed. This fellow had a whole wardrobe of smiles, more pretty than handsome, lithe and blond with those shard-blue eyes.

"I'm cold." My whole body was shaking, even my head.

"Won't be long now."

I shut my eyes against what lay ahead.

I could wake up and find out everything was fine, or at least, treatable. I'd smoked for the past thirty years—after a meal, a walk, or a swim, as a coda to making love, when I still had a lover, before bed, with my first cup of coffee. Nobody talks about the pleasure. As I lay on that table, I thought about how long it had been since I'd made love. What a beautiful phrase, *making* love! Could one *make* love? Maybe. I'd made love for those I cared about—Bella, Max, Levin—unlike my mother, who rationed it out like a miser counting and hoarding coins of gold. It had been over six years since I'd had sex. I'd taken to wearing tight bandage-like sports bras to conceal my full breasts and baggy slacks and sweaters to hide my long willowy arms and legs. More like bamboo sticks. I started laughing crazily, the painful chesty sounds turned into a coughing fit, eyes smarting tears.

The nurse was by my side, alarm in his eyes, a new smile of wonder and surprise. He handed me a tissue.

I wiped my eyes, and my hacking eased, then stopped. I'd had some suspicious test results, a positive CA 125, which was not always accurate—there were false positives. My ob-gyn found some swelling in my right ovary, and I'd had bloating, heartburn, and back pain. No news there.

The nurse explained that Dr. Silver was going to remove a tissue sample and some abdominal fluid unless he went in and found out he had to do more extensive surgery.

Modern medicine could do wonders, but in some areas we hadn't advanced much in the past decade. As a doctor, this was one thing I knew for sure.

"Dr. Silver will be with you soon."

"I have my own patients to think of...." My words trailed off.

His handsome head circled, a cross between yes and no. "Dr. Silver will want to discuss your results with you after the procedure."

I liked my gynecologic oncologist, a warm, caring, and elegant man, straight-backed, impeccably dressed. Like my father, Dr. S had a calling; he was kind and attentive to his patients, and it was clear he was doing what he was meant to do. Dr. Silver was golden. You can't fake it; patients can smell a phoney, just as children do.

Yet I was afraid. Not young, hardly old. Dreams and goals yet to pursue. Hungry for life, still. I had my children to think of, my patients.

Dr. Silver came in and patted my shoulder as the anesthesiologist dosed me up. My mind wandered far from the frigid white room and the sharp gleaming instruments that would penetrate my womb and its possibly diseased parts.

"Please stay as still as possible," a nurse said, and I willed my head to stop wagging, that crazy shaking, as if to say, *no, no, no!*

I drifted off. For a while, I heard the medical staff moving around me, the whir and clink of instruments, then I was floating in an aqueous world.

I rose up from the bottom of the sea, a lovely dreamworld. Heat spread through my abdomen, a beat like a pulse, distant, muffled in cotton. Dr. Silver's voice was calm and kind as he told me I had advanced ovarian cancer. He'd removed both ovaries, my Fallopian tubes, and uterus. "We're going to keep you here for a bit," he said, before laying out the treatment plan and follow-up, which he hoped would make me "more comfortable."

"Should I be making funeral arrangements?"

Dr. Silver sat with me for a long while saying little.

It had all happened so fast.

"How long do I have?"

He bowed his head, as if in prayer, then put a large, warm hand on my shoulder. "Miri, now is the time to figure out what matters to you most."

I felt myself burst into bloom.

III

I sat alone in my apartment, letting winter twilight flood in, the sky glowing midnight blue and a silver moon outside my window thin as a fingernail. Night seeped in and I refused to turn on a light. My answering machine blinked with messages and my cell beeped—text after incoming text—but their needy sucking force had no effect on me. I didn't want to see anyone, wasn't ready to share my week-old news with loved ones, friends, acquaintances, or strangers.

I was off OxyContin and on to milder palliatives. Goodbye to extreme nausea, dizziness, blurred vision, and rather terrifying hallucinations. Your experience was different, I later learned. You liked Oxy, a bit too much—you're not alone there. (But I didn't know anything much about you, yet.)

I poured myself a stiff scotch and lit a cigarette. Why deny myself simple pleasures? Mind you, there was a dark streak of relief in knowing the truth. And holding it fast within myself. Alone.

After two weeks at home, I told my children and a few close friends the bad news. Before my kids came up from New York and the rondo of Good Samaritans from Temple assailed me with gooey cards, poinsettias, ill-timed visits, and gloppy casseroles, I had a blessed window of time to myself. I drank and smoked and thought and asked myself questions.

How long have I got?

Where will I go?

What do I believe?

Can I leave something behind?

What is most important to me... now?

You see, my tumours were Grade 4, my cancer, Stage 3. Dr. Silver warned me against going on the internet and looking at survival rates, as many sites were out of date. I knew all about Kaplan-Meier curves, some like an airplane gently beginning its descent, others a dive-bomber.

Before my diagnosis, I knew I would die but I didn't know when. After my diagnosis, I knew I would die but I didn't know when. Not all that different from the vast human population.

But of course now it was different.

I was on a one-way road. But we were all going one way.

For years I'd experienced the twists and turns of that road, but not its dead end. The long and winding road.... I loved that Beatles song. I listened to it on continuous loop and cried, feeling sorry for myself, then sickened by all this self-pity.

I'd been recuperating at home for nearly seven weeks. By this time, Bella, Max, and the synagogue Samaritans had all gone home.

Suddenly I was alone. It was so quiet all I heard was the rush of cars on Tupper, a wet shushing sound not unlike ocean waves.

For the first time since my surgery, I found I was hungry, but I couldn't stand the thought of another defrosted casserole wedge. Hunger was hope, made me feel alive. My body was still good and it needed fuel. Cornucopie delivered and I called in my order and savoured the sensation of wanting, of appetite, hoping mine was hearty enough to stand up to a little tomato soup, a bit of bread and butter. While I waited, I changed into a pair of pajamas that my daughter Bella had bought me in a little shop on Greene Avenue that sold overpriced fancy socks, hosiery, and every type of girly gewgaw and tchotchke you could think of. The PJs were a warm fuzzy fleece, black with cavorting polar bears, something a teenager might wear. Slipping them over my bare skin, I sighed with pleasure. I never wanted to take them off. Twenty minutes later, the doorbell rang and there you were, brushing snowflakes off your parka.

I stood with my door partly ajar, hiding behind it. I could tell right away that you didn't remember me.

"Mrs. Gildener, your order from Cornucopie."

"*Dr.* Gildener." I knew I was being pretentious, or a flirt, but couldn't help myself.

"*Dr.*" You bowed dramatically and I laughed at myself, at you.

I reached for the bag and it nearly dropped from my trembling hands. You caught it just in time. "Let me take it into the kitchen for you."

I nodded as you removed your boots, pulling off the heel of one with the toe of the other, then kicking off the remaining boot with a socked heel.

"Thank you," I said, as you set the bag on the counter. I grabbed my purse, took out a toonie and loonie, and handed them to you. You waved away the tip. "Enjoy your evening, Dr. Gildener."

"How *are* you?" I asked.

You were nearly out the door, but turned to me, a cross between confoundment and surprise in your eyes, translucent against your olive skin.

"Still nothing green!" I called out.

You stepped back inside and joined me in the kitchen and I could see that at last you knew who I was. "No steak and chocolate this time?"

"I've lost my taste for both." I remembered what I'd said to you in the market, *I'm dying,* and what you replied.

We exchanged a smile. You're a handsome guy, but you have little vanity. I took notice of your face, its details—your sharply hewn cheekbones and determined chin, the clear grey eyes that had a glow of gold at their centres. Rough and weathered skin, a scar like the letter *z* on your left cheek, just missing the lower eyelid.

I was looking forward to the tomato soup, a bit of bread. The delivery had brought me back to life, to this dear world.

"Cup of tea?"

There was a small flicker as your eyes expanded and you glanced at your watch, then out the window for a moment before you said, "You're my last delivery."

I wasn't sure what that meant—did you want to get home to a wife, some kids? Then you added, "Sure, sounds good."

"Take your pick." I opened the cabinet to my neat row of silver canisters and coloured boxes. I felt a frisson of pleasure and surprise that you chose my favourite: lapsang souchong.

I set water to boil and fixed a pot of tea the old-fashioned way, heating it first with boiling water, putting tea leaves in a little silver brew basket that hooked over the side. We sat at my kitchen table as darkness filled the sky. I turned on another light.

"I don't even know your name."

"Guy Belvedere." You held out your hand and enclosed mine. "*Dr.* Gildener, good to meet you... officially."

"Miri, please. What are you doing at the market, Guy?" A car passed, its headlights silvering your eyes. "No, I mean, it's just that—"

Your head was thrown back and you were laughing. "You're a snob, Miri."

"No, no." I shook my head and poured the tea, a little ashamed of my tactless comment.

You added plenty of cream and sugar (though I find the smoky tea and milk mixture strange), then took a long pull as if it were a beer. "So I can think."

"About what?"

"My life."

"You sound like an old soul, ancient. You can't be forty."

"Correct."

I put out a good cheddar, some crackers, and a sliced green apple. "There you go, something green."

You reached for an apple slice and sandwiched it between thick chunks of cheddar. I saw your nicotine-stained fingers. "You smoke, I see."

"You see I'm *not* smoking."

"I'm craving a cigarette right now."

"You're a doctor."

"Indeed."

"What kind of doctor?"

"Psychiatrist."

"Wow. What's that like?"

"Travelling the world every day. Listening, trying to help. Being invisible. In a good way." I missed my practice, my patients. In fact, I missed everything about my usual life that, of course, I had taken for granted.

"Do you worry about all those messed up people? I mean, after hours."

I thought, *They don't need my worry.* "I'm there. I work with them so they can find their own way. That's the goal."

I appreciated that you didn't make a nasty crack. Your openness was unexpected, lovely. As I talked to you about my work, it was as if I saw it anew, through your eyes and ears as well as my own. Chatting with you brought me back to myself. And took me away too.

Hosting all the do-gooders, friends, and acquaintances had drained me dry. My children's visits had been hardest of all, the most painful. It was exhausting bearing the weight of their grief, buffering it. But you and I had no history. Being with you was easy and natural, a joy.

We talked for a few hours. It wasn't exactly what is condescendingly called "small talk," but it wasn't a rush of confessions either; there was no mad conversational stripping like two desperate strangers on a plane. Not at first, anyway. You were divorced, had a twenty-year-old son named Jean-François, used to work at a high school teaching music before becoming a trucker when you were unceremoniously laid off. You wanted to be closer to JF and talked about that for a while. How much JF had been through for a young man—he had lost his mother, Rachel, your ex Natalie's partner. You talked on for a bit, and I had a vague memory of a consultation, oh, maybe a couple of years before—two women who were very worried about their teenager who felt responsible for a young girl's death. It came back to me in more detail, but I couldn't say anything—professional confidentiality.

"He hates me," you were saying. "I was basically MIA."

"Because you were on the road? That must have been tough."

"Yeah, I guess. But I wasn't totally there when I was here. There and not there, you know?"

I nodded. Our conversation swerved. "You said something that day we collided in the market. Remember? When I said, 'I'm dying,' you shot back, 'Been there.'"

You drained your tea. "Got anything stronger?"

I went to my liquor cabinet and pulled out a bottle of Maker's Mark. "How about a hot toddy?"

"Bring it on."

I made us each one with bourbon and honey and wedges of lemon in stout little mugs. And thanks to your suggestion, I added cinnamon sticks, which I miraculously dug up in the back corner of the cupboard.

You cradled your hot toddy in both hands. "I'm lucky to be alive," you said, as cars shushed past with the sound of the sea. You were quiet for a moment or two and I glanced outside at the leftover snow, slushy and earth-streaked for the moment, and imagined I could almost smell spring, the air softer, shedding its edge of winter, buried beneath the debris and muck, shoots stirring in the dark.

IV

I was interested to learn more about your time hauling freight, driving an eighteen-wheeler for the Rosehill Group. That was your escape route, all those cross-border trips.

You often dreamed you were on the road again, driving that Mack, orange and white as a Creamsicle. Perhaps it was the sound of trains thundering through your neighbourhood in Saint-Henri, not far from my apartment on Tupper, but truly worlds apart. Passenger and freight trains racketed by day and night and you lived just a couple of blocks from the tracks. You didn't always relive the crash. Sometimes your dreams were good ones: bands of sunlight and shade rocking together at twilight while you slip-shifted through ten gears, natural as breath, or physical ones of hard sweat and grit, wrestling with a sixty-kilogram tarp, throwing straps, climbing atop a towering load of drywall in cold, wet, and muck as rain pounded down and a bungee cord popped off and snapped you in the head. Or crazy, funny ones, revisiting places you'd seen, like Fitzgerald, Georgia, with its clucking Burmese chickens running wild downtown. Some of your memories were heroic, reliving the night in Thunder Bay when you rescued a mongrel dog from the shoulder of the highway and took him to the vet the next morning, nursing him back to health. You adopted him, called him Atlas. Some of your memories were petty and embarrassing: driving eight hundred klicks with a miserable toothache or suffering jock itch so bad, bouncing and sweating in the driver's seat, that you sprayed some anti-fungal on your crotch at a rest-stop, or not bothering to stop at all and urinating into a jug. You dreamed in smells, sounds, and sensations, diesel, the rumble of the truck's powerful engine, the aroma of a summer night spent watching traffic pass as a cool wind caressed your face. Your memories were frustrating, arguing with a dumb dispatcher when you had to sit with your load all night in Hamilton because he'd failed to make an appointment for your delivery. Or spending the night in the terminal because you'd already exceeded your fourteen-hour clock and couldn't get back home till Sunday when you had to get on the road again that night, typical trucker's weekend.

Though I'd never been near a Mack, you made me feel like I was riding alongside you, made me understand the allure of long-distance trucking, why you had this lust for the road. You'd lived your whole life in Montreal, growing up in the Point. The caboose of seven kids, four boys and three girls, you lived in a housing development side by side with Irish folks, Poles, Ukrainians, Lithuanians, and *pure laine* French Canadians. I wasn't surprised to hear that you hadn't seen much beyond your own neighbourhood except for the occasional trip with the band when you were teaching high school music. Trucking was your chance to get out into the vastness of Canada and the US, and so had huge appeal. So did working alone. You were up to here with unimaginative principals and bottom-line budgets and school boards and interfering parents.

Big Joe's Trailer Truck! You'd made your mom read it to you over and over, just as Max made me read that same little book until my eyes and mind glazed over. (He still keeps a dog-eared copy in a crate that doubles as a nightstand beside his bed.) We followed Big Joe on a typical day's work in his giant trailer truck. Like you, Max loved the chart on the last two pages that labelled every single part of his rig.

CDL school surprised you. You expected a bunch of uneducated louts with tobacco-stained teeth who spoke mostly in swear words and slept in their denim and flannel. Instead you met an engineer, a former banker, and two women, one who'd been a nurse, the other a teacher.

You carried me away from myself, far from my sick body. I made more hot toddies for us both. I thought you didn't want to talk about the accident, but now that you'd started, you couldn't stop.

V

You were hauling a load of lumber down to Tennessee when it happened. It was late with clouds of hard blowing snow, impossible to see much of anything at all. You missed your turn-off, your mind wandering, thinking about your wife, Natalie, your ex at this point, and your boy, JF, who you were missing, missing them both, missing JF grow up. You liked some things about long-distance trucking, but there was lots you couldn't stand. The loneliness for one thing, the isolation. Must have been a wrong turn because now you were climbing up the Smoky Mountain Trail with hairpin turns and deep rocky drops that made your mouth parch and your stomach tumble. You climbed skyward up the mountain, and your dog Atlas curled under your seat, smelling trouble. There was a guard shack and the guy came out and told you that the road dead-ended at the top. You had no idea how the hell you were going to get down, no clue how to turn around. The Smoky Mountain Trail is not designed with eighteen-wheelers in mind. There was a little grassy area by the guard shack flanked by deep ditches. The snow was coming down harder now and you could barely get the Mack into gear or see much. As you were trying to manoeuvre the truck between those two ditches, a red Chevy thundered down from the peak and you swerved. The Chevy barrelled into you at top speed, and the Mack tumbled into the ditch and rolled over.

You slugged down the rest of your hot toddy and went quiet. I rested my hand on top of yours and felt you shake slightly, moving my hand with yours.

You thanked me, scribbled down your cell number, in case I ever needed anything, layered up, and went back out to your car.

I stayed awake a long while that night thinking about you. Surviving, you'd had a second birth. Your life divided into Before and After. Like me, now.

VI

I did the treatments designed to make me "more comfortable"—I considered it my job—then I had to recover. Finally, gratefully, I returned to work, part-time, and immersed myself in my practice. It was spring and Montreal had passed through the ugly winter-battered phase and was green and bursting with colour. Coming out of my isolation and winter's palette of grey, black, and white, the vivid hues of the flowers, even the cars, the greens—so many greens—pulsed. Ordinary tasks and activities gave me so much pleasure. Walking in Westmount Park, taking out a novel at La Grande Bibliothèque and sitting in the café for twenty minutes with a coffee and a pastry, just reading. I felt well enough to walk to the market, do my own shopping, and wheel my groceries home in a cart. Seeing you there was the highlight of my day. We were furtive, stealthy, barely spoke, like colleagues in the same office who were having a clandestine affair that everyone knew about, an open secret. Silly! Nothing had happened, they kept you very busy, and no one was particularly interested in you and me. One soft evening in May, you unexpectedly followed me out of the store and we stood for a few minutes on the street.

"How you doing, Miri?"

"I'm so well."

"Great." You put a hand on my shoulder. "I loved talking to you."

The L word startled me.

"Say, I have to get home to walk Atlas. Want to stop by later? I'm in Saint-Henri, not far."

I found your apartment later that evening at 3729 Ste-Émilie in an old two-storey brick building with pale blue-grey trim and a fleur-de-lys etching in the glass of the front door. Just around the block from your apartment, on Nôtre-Dame, cafés and restaurants squeezed in next to pawn shops. The neighbourhood was in flux, fancy condos going up everywhere you looked. Your bell was broken, so I knocked.

I heard Atlas barking and then the two of you came to the door. Atlas jumped up on me until you ordered him to sit, and after a couple more jumps, he ran around me in circles and leapt onto the couch. He was lean and wiry, black, brown, and cream with reddish-brown freckles on his snout. He had scars on his belly and thighs and his right front paw was now a stump. None of his wounds slowed him down. I sat next to Atlas, and as I petted him, he licked my hand and wrist, snuggling closer until his front paw and legs were strewn across my lap. I marvelled at his long reddish-brown eyelashes, I'd never noticed a dog's eyelashes before.

"He's a cuddler. If he bugs you, just push him away."

The licking was a bit much, but his warm body felt good.

"What can I get you? I'm having scotch."

"Second that."

You poured me a glass and then put on some music, moody melodies with bass and a high-energy guitarist.

"Who's this?"

"Interpol. Their debut album *Turn On the Bright Lights*. Really old at this point. But their lyrics are smart, never hackneyed. Their guitarist, Daniel Kessler, is a big talent, and I like their lead singer, Paul Banks, who's taken over bass since Carlos D. bailed."

I nodded, listening, not knowing much about what you were talking about. "I love music. I mostly listen to classical."

"I listen to music every night. I hear things now in this album I never noticed before, though I remember the streaks of sadness—well, to be honest, misery."

You got up and winced, a buckling in your left knee and you grasped the edge of the couch with both hands, putting your weight on your arms. I stood and swept an arm around your bent back, felt the spasm of pain pass from you and through me.

Bracing yourself against the side of the couch, you sat back down with stiff legs, abandoning whatever it was you'd gotten up to do.

"You were telling me about this band."

"Yeah, well they've got another album I really like, *El Pintor*. We can listen to that. They're coming up here, I want to go see them.

Maybe I'll ask JF, though who knows if our taste in music meshes—or if he'd want to be seen at a concert with his uncool dad."

A soft breeze blew in through the open window, billowing the yellowed lace curtains.

"It's a beautiful night," I said.

"I can show you our garden. It'll be light out for a bit."

We finished our drinks and headed outside with Atlas, who pulled hard on his leash.

On the opposite side of the street was a little *Jardin Communautaire* backed by a pale blue cement wall. A high wire mesh fence protected the garden and the entrance had a padlock hanging open. Green plastic tables and chairs were scattered here and there and small groups and couples were sitting outside, smoking and chatting. You greeted your neighbours and then showed me with obvious pride your individual plot, where you'd staked out some sort of bushy green plant. I've never had a green thumb and was not good at recognizing flowers or plants.

"I like the idea of growing something you can eat," you said.

Atlas nosed the fuzzy green leaves, took a nip.

"Hey!" You jerked his leash. "No!"

Atlas cowered, then sat at attention, looking up at you with doleful brown eyes.

"It's okay, boy. Tomatoes are risky, but if we get enough sun by late summer, hopefully I'll be picking some plump ripe red ones in August—if vandals don't get them first. Make a big salad or pasta sauce."

Someone had graffitied ONYX in shiny black spray paint on the far cement wall. "Don't forget to lock up," you called out to your neighbours, and they reassured you with nods and promises.

"We're right near the Lachine Canal," you said. "Up for a longer stroll?"

"Sure." I'd been cooped up in my apartment most of the winter and needed to build up my strength. I used to love walking and biking on the Lachine Canal in summer, spring, and fall. When Bella and Max were little, they took their inline skates or scooters and we made a day of it with a picnic on the green along with other families, people with whom our lives might never have intersected. It was such a nice feeling of community, being out here with my kids. It had been too long, but your stretch of the canal was another world from the area I was used to with its open green meadows and its sculpture garden.

In a moment, we passed by old and out-of-service train tracks along the south side of the Canal, which was thick with weeds. We walked by scrap yards and old containers painted pastel colours: pale green, pink, and yellow. Some of the containers were stacked three-high. The sky was a wash of blue with streaks of pearly clouds, the blossoming trees starting to silhouette against the sky, which looked like it had been painted with a brush. It was windy along the water, but the underside of the breeze was gentler, softer against our faces.

When you took my arm, the fresh air and the blood pumping in my legs cleared my mind and brightened my spirit. I fell into your slightly lopsided rhythm, a long stride with the right foot, a slower dragging of the left.

"I'm supposed to walk an hour a day," you told me, "so I don't lose mobility. I'm pretty bad about it."

"It's hard to find time, I guess."

The old painted containers had a charm and beauty all their own. Soon we passed a red caboose with white graffitied initials painted on its black-boarded windows.

The water rushed past—rippling with the wind, a brilliant blue— as the early spring twilight drew into a gloaming.

We walked for a half hour, maybe forty minutes. It was dark by then, the moon full and orange, bright as a pumpkin, sending flickers of golden light across the river.

All at once, I felt a weariness seep into my legs, a pulsing ache. I slowed, then stopped. Atlas hovered near me.

"You okay?"

"I haven't gotten much exercise in a while. Best to go back."

"Sure." You encircled my arm tighter, your hand at my hip, steadying me.

Blessedly we came upon a bench and I sank into it with a long sigh. You stayed close beside me. The wind picked up and felt chillier now that we were still, but I needed to rest. Once I sat for a while, how the hell would I get up?

"I'm worried about getting back."

You turned to me. "This was a stupid idea. Sorry."

"No, no. It's wonderful to be out."

"I can always carry you piggyback."

"Right. I'm a sylph."

"Yeah, I see that."

"I'm dying, Guy. This time for real." My words were shots in the quiet dark.

You didn't say anything.

"I'm on this little island now," I went on, "black water lapping all around me."

You nodded.

"Back to work part-time, doing some normal things, but it won't last." I told you about my diagnosis, about the surgery and treatments I'd been through. "I may not have much time. Can't get my doctors to give me the straight dope."

"I know how that goes."

"I need to make some decisions. Soon. I can't really confide in my kids. They get too upset. I don't want to burden them any more than—"

"What can I do?"

I leaned into your shoulder and sidled closer for warmth and comfort. You put both arms around me in a sheltering sweep and we sat until I could work up the strength to get up again and make our way back, achingly slow, but on my own two feet.

VII

My island stayed safe through a very short spring and most of that sultry summer, though I was weak, weary, and often in pain. On a late August day when it seemed I breathed vapour instead of air and the muggy sun shone through heavy clouds, Dr. Silver told me that my cancer had spread to my spine. That explained my persistent backache, being bone tired. Literally.

Death. Its reality splayed out its black silhouette, gaslighting, shadowing me.

The following week, I saw each of my remaining patients and said goodbye, absorbing their grief and tears, as I wrote down the name and contact number of the trusted colleague I was referring them to. That settled, I had to face my kids, who, thankfully, were not kids anymore. But still.

Max and Bella were arriving in Montreal together for the weekend. I was dreading their visit, and I girded myself up with long talks and short walks with you, lubricated by plenty of scotch and—I should be more embarrassed to say—lots of cigarettes.

I prepared as if I were having a party—elegant little sandwiches, a pot of coffee, and a selection of pastries. Max, burly and bearded, paced around my apartment, and Bella, way too thin with her wild masses of wheat-coloured hair, stationed herself in a hard-backed chair armed with a notebook and a selection of perfectly sharpened pencils, some of them coloured.

"Max, darling, please sit down. You're making me nervous."

I went to the couch and motioned them over. I offered food and drink, but nobody wanted anything.

"First, tell me your news. Max, how's the restaurant going?"

"Do we have to talk about that? Now? Today?" He tugged on his beard which was very scruffy.

"What about you, Bella? How're you doing?"

"Okay," Bella said in her no-nonsense voice. "I'm auditioning for the lead in *Betrayal.*"

"My favourite Pinter."

"It's got a great director," Bella said. "I love her work."

"When is your audition?"

"Next week."

"Call me, Bella. Let me know how it goes. How's business at Chez Max? Fill me in."

"Busy," Max said, encouraged by his sister. "We can't offer enough poutine and people are ordering Bretons by the dozens. It's hard to keep up. Oh, and we've gotten requests for a bagel, bacon, and peanut-butter toasted sandwich."

"I'd order that," I said.

"Well, I'm not putting it on the menu. It would offend some of my clients."

"You could use smoked meat instead of bacon," I offered, enjoying the pleasures of an ordinary conversation rather than life or death talk.

"Gross," said Bella.

"Wouldn't be the same."

"If no one is going to have anything to eat, I certainly will. Shame to waste all this."

I helped myself to coffee, a few smoked salmon and cream-cheese sandwiches, and a miniature apple pastry. I ate, balancing the plate on my lap, and brought them up to date on my health, or lack thereof.

No one spoke for what felt like a full five minutes. I set my plate on the coffee table. I could see my son crying silent tears, not bothering to wipe them, as they soaked into his unkempt beard. I went to him and sat very close, wiping the wet away gently with a tissue and putting my arms around his shoulders, kissing his forehead.

"I know, love, I know."

Bella's skin was very pale and her long fingers shook as she took up her pad and one of the sharpest pencils. Red.

"Mom," she said, "I'm going to make some appointments. I want to get a second, maybe a third opinion. I know in this day and age something can be done. It's impossible to believe that—"

"Stop. Please." I held my hands up, palms facing her.

"What do you mean?"

"Just what I said. I don't want any more medical interventions. You need to respect my wishes."

"Mom! How can you give up so easily? You're young, too young...."

She went on, her voice loud and strident, but the words had no more meaning to me than a cloud of mosquitoes buzzing around my ears.

I heard Max say, "Shut up, Bella."

But she rattled on and I rose from the couch and shut myself into my bedroom, just as she'd done as a teenager.

Soon she was rapping on the door. I hadn't locked it and she walked in and sat on the edge of the bed where I was lying on my back. Max settled on my other side.

"I'm sorry, Mommy," Bella said. "I don't want to lose you."

Max was weeping. "What will I do if I miss you? *Mom?*"

I sat up and put an arm around each of them and we cuddled like that on my bed as if they were toddlers and had both had nightmares. "Talk to me. You both have my voice inside you forever."

It was a long, long weekend. I wanted to talk to you, but I felt I needed to devote everything I had to Max and Bella, who needed me much more.

We finally got around to my wishes. DNR. No, I did not want to be buried in Mount Hebron Cemetery in Queens along with all my other relatives. We discussed my being cremated at greater length than I had ever anticipated, even though I knew the conversation was irrelevant. Bella took a lot of notes—it was all that kept her from completely falling apart or becoming enraged with me. Max, my baby, was stunned, sad, and tender-hearted. I worried more, as always, about him. Bella was tough, but there was something fragile in my boy. When they finally left and I collapsed back in bed, I was so relieved to reach you right away. You came over. I never doubted your promise to check in on both of my children and make sure they were all right. You lay beside me on my bed, just as my father had done every night of my childhood, until I fell asleep. In the morning you were still there.

VIII

We left together for Key West shortly after my children's visit because I knew I didn't have much time before I would be too ill to travel. During the previous few weeks, I'd discovered how organized you could be when you wanted to be. I know it will serve you in good stead, whatever you decide to do next. The B&B was reserved, the car and boat all rented ahead of time. Lucky for us, your ex agreed to take Atlas—JF promised to come home directly after work to walk him.

I felt euphoric as our plane picked up speed and rose magically into the air, a lift in my belly, a soaring in my heart, as I saw the world spread out below—the cars and parks and people just playthings, tiny coloured toys—before we glided through the endless expanse of puffy white clouds. As if it were my first time on a plane. Which it wasn't. I reached for your hand and you interlaced your fingers with mine. We didn't need to speak.

As you pulled the rental car out of the Miami airport for the drive down to the southernmost point in the mainland US, you said, "So. Key West, eh?"

"End of the line."

"And?"

"Supposed to be beautiful. Never been, neither have you."

The drive took us along Overseas Highway, and we passed through some forty or more little islands en route. I felt like a little girl, gazing out the open window, the Atlantic Ocean on one side, a dark roiling blue, and the Gulf of Mexico, calmer, a lighter brighter royal, on the other. When I tired, or my back ached from too much sitting, we stopped and I lay across the back seat and napped, lulled by the salt air and rhythm of constant motion. Though it was summer, the sea breezes were cool and refreshing.

About halfway there, after our stop at a Cuban deli for *café con leche* and coconut cookies, you were happy to have me back up front, the coffee and rest having revived me. Alongside the highway, the sea turned into many shades of green: emerald, turquoise, and teal. You concentrated on your driving, but I couldn't help pointing out a beautiful heron and then a wheel of crows overhead. You held my hand as you drove.

My mood turned as we pulled into the town of Key West. The streets were narrow and clotted with people, cyclists, and cars like ours, which had no room to manoeuvre.

"What we really need here are bikes," I said absurdly, as if I would ever ride a bike again.

You didn't answer, concentrating on getting us to our B&B as quickly as possible. The heat and noise were terrible. A cluster of tourists with bulging backpacks waddled past souvenir shops, eating what looked like giant pieces of fluffy key lime pie on paper plates, cotton candy, or stuffed their faces, picking from greasy white bags of fried foods. There were raggedly dressed bums and drunks and poor souls who rocked and shook with the riot of their own unrelenting voices.

I had no patience or charitable feeling for anyone and refused to feel ashamed of my own bad attitude. I'd spent my whole life being brutally self-critical. Enough. You closed the windows and turned on the AC. I didn't know what I'd been expecting. Anything but this.

"We'll be at the place soon. Hang in there."

I closed my eyes as we crawled toward the B&B. At last you pulled up in front of a large, gracious white-pillared house with a shaded veranda on a quiet side street in the Old Town.

When you helped me out of the car, my legs were so stiff that they nearly buckled, and it took a few minutes to get myself steady, then mobile. You took my arm and led me through the lobby and into the office. The woman who checked us in was chatty and wanted to give us a truckload of information.

"We're pretty fried," you broke in, as she was explaining something about pool towels and a wine bar where you needed to use a special card. She described our room, which was up a flight of stairs, apparently.

"Anything on the ground floor?" Guy asked.

"I'm sorry, no."

We took our keys and made our way over to the room, which was in the carriage house. The grounds were tranquil and lovely with a pool glittering aquamarine under lanterns, and beyond, an acre of tropical gardens.

Our room had a private entrance, and with painfully slow steps, we made our way up to the second floor. It was spacious with a vaulted ceiling and a private veranda overlooking the pool and gardens. The ceiling fan whirred slowly, casting light and shadow on the bare pine floor, a four-poster bed of mahogany and a lovely antique writing desk. I went into the washroom which had a marble bath and Jacuzzi tub. I hoped I'd feel strong enough to luxuriate in there, with a little help from you to get me in and out without cracking my skull open or breaking any fragile bones.

We held hands and did a little jig, laughing together.

"So, what do you want to do first? Tired?"

"Always."

"I need a walk after all that driving. Why don't you rest and I'll check out the area, get everything organized for tomorrow. We can stroll around later. How's that sound?"

"Perfect." I had my eye on the lovely little desk—I wanted to write a note to Bella and one to Max, not to mention you. I felt this urgency to get down on paper the history of us.

IX

I fix myself a cup of mint tea and go to the writing desk, still in my travelling clothes. There is a supply of thick cream-coloured stationery embossed with green palm trees and two pens with green ink—the colour of life. Settling into the hard-backed chair, I begin a letter to Max as an ache throbs in my lower back, shooting lightning rays of agony into my abdomen and down my legs. This chair with its carved mahogany back and shapely legs has morphed into an instrument of torture.

I build a fortress of pillows on the bed—several behind my back and one beneath my knees—and place a fentanyl patch on my lower back. I go on writing and writing until I nod off.

Some hours later, I hear you come in and slowly open my eyes, propping myself up on my elbows.

"Hey, sleeping beauty, how're you doing?"

"Not too terrible."

"This place is amazing."

"I think I feel up to a walk around. Give me a minute to get ready."

You pour each of us a sparkling water and head out to our veranda while I struggle to get dressed. I am painstakingly slow. What was I thinking? I had packed a pretty dress and a beautiful new bathing suit, a black forties-style maillot, which highlights my miraculously well-preserved breasts, the only part of my body that hasn't shrunk and curdled with cancer. I slip on my blue linen shift and a cropped white cardigan with delicate pearl buttons, then struggle to buckle strappy white sandals before joining you on the veranda, the perfect place to people watch.

Couples and singles are sitting around the pool and strolling in the gardens. Tables arranged near the bar are filled with pairs and small groups. I'm grateful that this isn't a rowdy place. In fact, most of the people are older than us—silver-haired seniors—though there are several stylish gay couples, their tight t-shirts showcasing muscular biceps, well-toned chests, and abdomens.

You take me in. "You look nice."

I can't contain the smile that spreads across my face as warmth floods my cheeks.

"Ready?"

We make our way down the stairs, your arm around me, though you are not all that steady yourself. Passing the bar and pool, we head into the lush tropical gardens. A white-painted gazebo is lit golden and there are two pairs of fashionable men in black jeans and fedoras drinking something pale gold and bubbly, laughing and talking, maybe celebrating an occasion. A winding path leads through dense palms, some shaped like an open Chinese folding fan, as well as a ficus with aerial roots dense and braided as plaits of hair. In a little pond, two giant tortoises loll, one partly covered by a palm leaf. I sit on a stone bench, and you join me, both of us surrounded by blooms.

You know your plants, flowers, and trees, and you point out purple and fuchsia orchids with gold and cream centres, a bleeding heart with crimson and pink petals. Something called a fishtail palm with elongated green leaves in the shape of a metal chain. You show me ginger blooms shaped like pinecones and flame vines that creep up a fence, bleeding it bright orange. We rest for a few minutes, watching the absolute stillness of the tortoises, and then amble on through the maze of paths. A parrot perches on a branch, surrounded by pale and hot pink blooms shaped like old-fashioned powder puffs. So much lush life makes me long for it to go on, long to get beyond longing.

As if you can read my thoughts, you take my hand as we wander, lingering in the gardens. When it is full dark, we go into the wine bar. It's set up so that with a special card, we can order a one-ounce taster or a full glass of any of some three dozen wines. If we really love a particular wine, bottles are kept in stock for purchase. The selection is daunting.

We sample a red—rich and full-bodied, slightly fruity and woodsy—and then some thinner, more acidic reds. Our first taste, a wine called Tribute (how apt), is our favourite, and you buy a bottle. We have it opened right away and then wander over to the gazebo with the bottle and a couple of glasses.

The others have left, so we have the place to ourselves now. As you pour each of us a glass of wine, you look at me, searching. "How're you feeling?"

"Too good."

We clink glasses without making a toast right away.

"*L'Chaim*," I say at last. Yes, I can toast to life. For you, my children, myself. I love this life.

Soon I'm pleasantly tipsy. I babble and you go quiet.

"I think we should eat," you insist.

But when I try to get up, I nearly go down, feeling like sand in an avalanche but you steady me just in time.

"I'll go rustle up some dinner. You rest."

Somehow we make it back up the stairs, and I return to my pillow fort and my writing—a letter to Max, one to Bella, and one for you. Urgency gives me unexpected stamina.

When you return with provisions and another bottle of wine, a white Sancerre this time, we unpack the food from Blue Heaven— *yes, of course that's where I want to go*—and I think of how many teas and coffees and scotches and wines and snacks and meals we've shared since we met and got to know one another. Talks and walks and sustenance.

I help you lay out our feast on the veranda. There is jerk chicken with peas and rice and fried plantains for you and a filet of salmon in a coconut sauce with white rice and some crispy kale sprinkled on the top for me. A wedge of cornbread, still warm, and an enormous slice of that fluffy and ubiquitous key lime pie to share.

You dig in and I pick at my plate. The salmon is delicious, the coconut sauce sweet and creamy, but I can only consume little bites. I sip the wine, crisp and tangy, a perfect complement to the spicy food.

We share a cigarette, back and forth, mouth to hand, hand to mouth. We stay up ridiculously late talking.

"I'm dying (ha-ha) to try that bathtub." Yes, I crave water more than anything now, baths, pools, seas, waves.

I undress and run the bath very warm, pouring in scented sea salts. You knock, and when I say okay, you come in.

"Don't look."

You help me in and then quietly shut the door.

I soak, eyes closed, blissful.

And then I hear you come in and offer to wash my back, my downy baby bird tufts of hair. I dunk underwater once and then again, just to feel its silky warmth everywhere.

Afterward you lift me from the bath and carry me to the bed, one arm around my back, the other beneath my dangling legs.

I feel unexpectedly good, a melting heat, and a little loopy from the wine and meal. I take out a raspberry-coloured fentanyl lollipop.

"Want a lick?" I lift the sheet, pat the space beside me.

You strip off your clothes, your body muscular and scarred and so beautiful to me now. You lay on your side, cradling me in your arms.

"Who am I to you?" I ask.

You stroke my cheek, not saying anything.

Leaning your face into mine, your bristling cheek against my cheek, your hair's gone long and unruly, smelling like the pelt of an animal.

"Soon, very soon I will not be." I go on gamboling in soliloquy, high on good food and wine and my meds and you and me and life itself.

"No, no, not that," you say, holding your ears.

"What, you don't like *Hamlet*? Even butchered by me?"

"I was tortured with that play... back in college. And a few of his others. Everyone ends up dead."

"That's how it goes." I lick my painkilling lolly, then lay it on the nightstand.

"C'mere."

With great gentleness, you turn and pull me against you, your chest and belly and thighs spooning around me, your arms rubbing my shoulders, caressing my breasts as you kiss the back of my neck.

Desire takes me by surprise, and I turn slightly, my arms above my head, my face buried into the pillow as you enter me, moving slowly, deeply, then quickening your rhythm, your fingers stroking, plucking, playing my body like your instrument until I cry out in pain and pleasure. This is our first time. Our last.

I didn't know I could still come. Now, soon, I will go. You fall asleep spooning me and I am wide awake, here, unbearably happy.

On the boat, chugging along in the twilight, I will be frightened all of a sudden, shivering and slick with sweat. You will zip me into your hoodie as we head toward the reef, the sun lowering in the sky until it nearly sinks into the sea.

Perhaps we'll spot a cormorant, huge, with an orange-yellow bill and black neck, spreading its wings and flying over the water. A pelican diving for his dinner.

I won't just wither. My terminal illness is interminable to the people who love me, who are not dying—not yet. I won't do that to my children and I won't do that to you. I will not do that to me.

Death will come to me like waves to the sea, like the birth of each of my kids, and I'll ride those fucking breakers of pain so close to joy, going one way, no stopping now until the climax of delivery. Deliverance.

You'll dither, heading our boat into the mangroves with their rank smell of overripe life. In the mudflats, we'll see a flamingo, pink and white on stilt legs with a hooked bill, like a magic creature in a fairy-tale.

At last we'll arrive at our reef, the waters nearly turquoise, glittering in the setting sun like a bed of aquamarines.

You'll stop the boat and help me get on my fins. Then I'll take out my stockpile of benzos, and with a slug of water, I'll swallow them all. A few pills, dry and pasty, will stick in my throat. So I'll drink more water, again and again, until they all go down. I'll try out the snorkelling mask and breathing tube and feel a momentary shard of dread, panic that I've gone through with this, no way back, done it. And then a wash of relief.

It's okay, it'll be all right.

Now I see and feel everything that will happen, how I'll go.

I'll lower my mask as you help me down into the water and quickly follow.

There is such utter quiet—just the whoosh of my own breathing. You swim beside me. I kick softly so as not to disturb the underwater life. What life exists below! Large white fish speckled with gold polka dots. Listen! There is a strange low grunting, a vibration, as a school of fish with orange-and-blue stripes ripples by. A creature scours the ocean floor with barbs overturning the sand, searching for food. A cave, fish darting in and out, thin tails like swords.

THE SLEEP OF APPLES

We are among them, breathing underwater. My heart is bursting, mind floating free.

Stray thoughts. How can you not forgive? Know you are not abandoned. Asleep midafternoon, morning, and night, rain falling on the waves, the sea, open, the whole sky is ours.

ACKNOWLEDGEMENTS

I'm grateful to the Banff Centre for Arts and Creativity for time, space, and mentorship. Thanks to Alex Leslie and Zsuzsi Gartner who both helped me strengthen this book. I was fortunate to have a residency in the Boat, one of the Leighton Artists Studios at Banff, to work on *The Sleep of Apples* during a May snowstorm among the mountains, woods, and elk.

Heartfelt thanks to the Virginia Center for the Creative Arts (VCCA), where the quiet and companionship of several residency fellowships among wonderful writers, artists, and composers enabled me to complete *The Sleep of Apples*.

Grateful thanks to Renée Knapp and the wonderful team at Inanna Publications. I'm inspired by, and indebted to, the late, great editor-in-chief, Luciana Ricciutelli, for all she offered me and her authors, as well as her immeasurable contribution to women's publishing. She is greatly missed.

I appreciate the editors of the literary journals who championed these stories and gave them their first home in the world.

Walks and bike rides along the Lachine Canal through many seasons over many years inspired these stories. *The Sleep of Apples* is a love song to my home city: Montreal.

Remembering and honouring my late mother Dr. Minette P. Davis who told me a story near the end of her life that set my fiction antennae buzzing and resulted in *The Sleep of Apples*.

For those who face mortality far too soon.

For those who grapple with mental illness and get through yet another day.

For those beautiful human fish who swim every which way and do not fit into column A or column B.

Finally, to Michael, Tobias, and Gabriel. Your love and belief sustain me.

The author wishes to thank the following publications in which some of these stories first appeared:

The Jewish Literary Journal: "What's Mine Is Yours"

Plenitude: "The Arrangement"

Drash: "Devotion"

Montréal Serai: "Will the World Pause for Me?", "Tracks," and "How Did This Become My Life?"

The New Quarterly: "Male and Female Created He Them" and "The Sleep of Apples"

Bellevue Literary Review: "Brother's Keeper"

Photo credit: Monique Dykstra, Studio Iris

Ami Sands Brodoff is the award-winning author of three novels and two volumes of stories. Her latest novel, *In Many Waters,* grapples with our worldwide refugee crisis. *The White Space Between,* which focuses on a mother and daughter struggling with the impact of the Holocaust, won The Canadian Jewish Book Award for Fiction (The Vine Award). *Bloodknots,* a volume of thematically linked stories, was a finalist for the ReLit Award. Ami leads creative writing workshops for teens, adults, and seniors. She has also taught writing to formerly incarcerated women and to people grappling with mental illness. Ami has been awarded fellowships to Yaddo, the Banff Centre for Arts and Creativity, Virginia Center for the Creative Arts, Ragdale Foundation, and St. James Cavalier Arts Centre for Creativity (Malta). Learn more at amisandsbrodoff.com.

Also by Ami Sands Brodoff

Can You See Me?
The White Space Between
Bloodknots
In Many Waters